JOHN CROWLEY

T0161917

PM PRESS OUTSPOKEN AUTHORS SERIES

PM PRESS OUTSPOKEN AUTHORS SERIES

TOTALITOPIA

plus

"This Is Our Town"

and

"Everything That Rises"

and

"Paul Park's Hidden Worlds"

and

"I Did Crash a Few Parties"
Outspoken Interview

and much more

PM PRESS | 2017

"Totalitopia" first appeared in *Lapham's Quarterly*, Fall 2011

"And Go Like This" and "Gone" appeared in Crowley's *Novelties & Souvenirs: Collected Short Fiction*, HarperCollins, 2004

"In The Tom Mix Museum" was originally published in *This Land*, July 15, 2012

"Everything That Rises" is from the "Easy Chair" column, *Harper's*, January 2016

"Paul Park's Hidden Worlds" is from the *Boston Review*, May/June 2016

"This Is Our Town" is original to this volume

ISBN: 978-1-62963-392-3
Library of Congress Control Number: 2016959589

Outsides: John Yates/Stealworks.com
Author photograph by Misha Nazarenko
Insides: Jonathan Rowland

PM Press
P.O. Box 23912
Oakland, CA 94623
www.pmpress.org

10 9 8 7 6 5 4 3 2 1

Printed in the USA by the Employee Owners of Thomson-Shore in Dexter, Michigan
www.thomsonshore.com

CONTENTS

This Is Our Town

WHEN I WAS YOUNG I lived in a place called Timber Town. It can be found in a book called *This Is Our Town*, which is part of the "Faith and Freedom" series of readers, and was written by Sister Mary Marguerite, SND (which stands for Sœurs de Notre-Dame) and published by Ginn and Company, copyright 1953. Catholic children read it in the fourth and fifth grades.

Timber Town was a small river town, where exactly the book never said, but it would have to be somewhere in the Northeast, maybe in Pennsylvania. Upriver from Timber Town was a place called Coalsburg, which was where the trains from the mines came down to load their coal onto barges. Downriver from Timber Town was a city of mills called Twin City, because a part of the city was on one side of the river and another, poorer part was on the other side. These names were easy to remember and understand, even for young children. River ferries and trains ran from town to town and farther, down somewhere to the sea I suppose. In the double title page you can see us kids high on a hillside, looking over the river valley and the mills and the church. We wear the saddle shoes and the striped shirts and flaring flowered skirts we did wear then, and in the pale sky are pillowy clouds and the black check-marks of flying birds. I can still feel the wind.

The book tells stories of then and now, of the flood that hurt so many houses in Timber Town and nearly washed away Coalsburg: I saw all that, I was there. The book has stories of long-before, when miracles happened to children like us in other lands, and stories of saints like St. John Bosco, after whom our school was named. But most of the stories are about our town, and the nuns in our school, and the priests in the church, and the feast days and holidays of the months one after another. The stories are all true and of course they happened to us or we caused them to happen, or they wouldn't be in the book; but the book never told everything about us, nor all that we could do and did.

*　*　*

May 1953
It has been a long time now since I last saw my guardian angel. Of course I know she's here with me all the time whether I can see her or not, and I can hear myself tell myself the words she would once say to me to guide me and keep me from harm, but I haven't seen her as herself, the way I guess all kids can.

I remember how she stood behind me at my First Communion, her hand on my shoulder, and how it was the same for all of us in white kneeling at the rail as the priest came closer to us, going from one to the next. We never talked about when or how we saw our guardian angels but we all knew. My brother Thad walked along beside the priest, in his cassock, with his hand on his breast, carrying the little tray on a stick (the *paten* he told me it's called) to hold under our chins as Father Paine placed the Host on our tongues, in case some tiny fragment of the Body of Christ fell off, because every fragment of the Host is God, at least for a while. Perhaps because it was the first time, we didn't feel—at least I didn't—the wondrous warmth and sweetness, the dark power too, that comes with swallowing God. It would come gradually, and we would long for it.

After Mass was done we all went out into the sun and the trees in flower and marched—or went in procession anyway—around the church to the white statue of Mary, crowned the previous Sunday with pink roses that had shed petals all around the statue's base. I never much liked this statue, white as the plaster casts in the library, her eyes unable to see. And there we sang.

My white dress and my little white missal and my white kid gloves were all put away and I was sitting on the back steps wearing dungarees, my feet bare, and she said (my guardian angel) that a sad thing about being an angel is that you can never partake of Communion like living people can. Angels know that it is a wonderful thing and they can know what their person feels, because they know their person and they know God. But they can never have it themselves.

I asked: Does that make an angel sad?

Well, my angel said, nothing *really* makes an angel sad.

And then she clutched her knee in her linked hands, just the way you do when you're sitting with crossed legs, and said There are angels for other things than people. Every animal in the world has a kind of angel, a little one or a big one, who's born with the animal and vanishes away when the animal dies.

Will you vanish away? I asked, but she laughed the way she does and said I am yours forever and will always be with you.

She doesn't have wings, and a long time ago when we were younger I asked her why. I don't need wings to come and go, she said. The pictures only show us with wings because that's the only way people can think of us, able to ascend and descend, run messages, see to the whole wide world. But big feathery wings or little wings stuck to their backs—who could ever fly with those?

I thought about that and about how birds' wings are their arms really.

Does Cousin Winnie have a guardian angel? I asked. Cousin Winnie wasn't a Catholic and didn't say prayers or go to any church.

Of course he does.

What is Cousin Winnie's guardian angel like?

Just like me. But older and . . . quieter. Actually I don't know what he's really like.

He can't see his guardian angel, I said. Can he?

Well you know what? my angel said. Grownups can't, mostly. Can't see or hear them.

They can't?

Not mostly.

I thought then that that was the saddest thing I had ever learned. And now I know it's so.

June

My mother wasn't born a Catholic. She went to many different churches, she said, and in school she learned to play the organ, and sometimes played in the churches her family went to. They moved a lot from town to town until she came to Timber Town and met Dad. Sometimes I think she was the only person in Timber Town who wasn't Catholic; but when she married Dad of course she had to become a Catholic, and she did, and she was glad about everything we did and the holidays and the feast days coming like chapters in their turn. But the one thing she went on loving were the hymns and the music in the churches she'd grown up in. And because she sang them in her soft voice as she worked or cooked, we learned them too; at least I did. She sang *Abide with me, fast falls the eventide* and she sang *Jesu, joy of man's desiring* and *Praise God, from whom all blessings flow* and I sat in silence and listened, and the words and the music entered my heart and still remain there.

She had a way of talking about things like saints and hymns and Bible quotes that made it seem she thought they were not serious or important to her, that they were like funny old poems or Bing Crosby songs, but I think that was because she actually loved them and wanted to protect them. She called the Thursday of Holy Week Maundy Thursday (we pretended she'd said Monday Thursday, and laughed every time, every year) and she knew of saints we hadn't heard of. Like St. Swithin. If it rains on St. Swithin's Day in June, she said, it will rain for forty days; and if the sun shines it will shine for forty days. He was also the patron saint of apples. She would sing:

> High in the Heavenly Places
> I see Saint Swithin stand.
> His garments smell of apples
> And rain-wet English land.

Mom's cousin Winnie came to stay with us now and then—when he had to rest, she said. We were told to call him Cousin Winnie as she did, even though he was older than Mom and I don't know whose cousin he really was. I also didn't know what he did in the world or what he had to rest from, but I do now. He would arrive weak and thin and shaking and be put into the little room at the top of the house and my mother would take care of him, though I was never sure she really liked him that much. He was a dim sort of person, at least when he was resting. When he got stronger he would help around the house. One thing he was good at was card tricks. He told us the Devil had taught him, and that's why we could never see through his tricks, but I don't think he believed in the Devil any more than he believed in God.

When he came to rest in our house for the last time he did none of those things. He didn't get up at all. When I brought him coffee in the morning it seemed he had been crying. He was gray-white like the worn old sheets he lay on.

I told Mom he was dying. I was sure of it, and my guardian angel was sure of it too. And I said she should call Father Michaels to come. Father Michaels is the parochial vicar and helps Father Paine. Cousin Winnie's not a Catholic, she said. But I knew what I knew and I just looked at her and looked at her until she went to the telephone.

Father Michaels came and talked with him a long time with the door of the little room shut. We waited in our rooms or in the kitchen and didn't make a sound. Cousin Winnie died a little while later.

I asked Mom: Did Father Michaels win his soul?

Well I don't know, my mother said. Winnie said a prayer at the end. And crossed himself. So I don't know.

Did he make a good act of contrition? I asked, because no sin can be forgiven without that.

Well, my mother said. He had a lot of sins to recount, and I doubt he got to all of them.

Then he would only go to Purgatory.

Uh-huh, my mother said, and even though she was crying she was laughing too. You bet. For a good long time too.

July

In the book *This Is Our Town* there are more chapters about the great flood than about anything else. It nearly washed away my house and other houses, and did wash away houses of miners and other people in Coalsburg; their houses came down the river in parts and pieces, roofs and fences and once a doghouse with a little goat riding on top of it. My brother went out with his friends in the fireman's rescue boat and rescued the goat. Along Second Street, which runs along the river, the water reached the windows of the first floors and kept rising. The gas and electricity stopped and we lived by lamps and candles and ate from cans. There is a chapter about how Mr. Popkin refused to take his ferry out for fear it would be swamped and lost. There is a chapter about how Father Michaels went up the river with an old man in a little motorboat to bring the Blessed Sacrament to the man's friend, who was dying. It's very dangerous, the man warns Father Michaels. *We will not think about danger*, Father Michaels replies. *My life would be worth nothing if I am afraid to save others for Christ.*

And then the Church of Saints Peter and Paul, our church, began to sag to one side as the earth and stones were washed away along the bank where it stood. It was decided that the school children should be taken to Twin City and stay in shelters made in the big school and the parish hall, sleep on cots, and go to Mass in the huge dark church there. We were among strangers.

The sisters who taught at St. John Bosco had come too and shared rooms with the Sisters of St. Joseph in their convents, and they came to the big church to Mass and to the special services held to pray for an end to the flood. It was like a big engine had doubled its power. Not all nuns are smart, and not all nuns are good; I knew that even then. But all of them have the power that God grants to all of us to bring about what we desire and need, and that power is greater in them. It's like the difference between the Twin City ball team and the Yankees.

This was for us to know: prayer is how the world is managed. The Epistle to the Thessalonians says *Rejoice always, and pray without ceasing*. I prayed at night before I went to sleep and in school before classes. I prayed when I walked and when I waited. I prayed in prayers I knew as well as my own name, and I prayed in my own words: that Dad could keep his job in Twin City in the machine shop where he cut gears—I didn't know what that meant but Dad loved his job, and though it seemed the shop would fail I prayed as hard as I ever had and it didn't fail. I prayed that Mom would stop smoking Old Golds because they aren't good for your lungs, and though I never told her I was praying for it there came a day when she stopped. She never said a thing about it, just stopped forever; later on when cleaning the living room she came upon an old pack half-empty and looked at it a long time as though she couldn't remember what it was.

Prayer isn't for things, Sister Rose of Lima told us. Prayer is attention: to God, to the soul, to the Virgin, to our hearts. Praying is for help to those in need, strength and courage for ourselves, honor and thanks to God. But I knew, and I knew she knew, that it was for things too: you had only to pray for something and receive it to know that. *Ask, and it shall be given you; seek, and you shall find; knock, and it shall be opened to you.* God made that promise to His Church and He can't take it back. Father Paine said that if we pray for what will harm us or harm others God must give us that too—though it may come in a form we don't recognize, and won't like. There must be a whole bureaucracy in heaven that is managing these things, putting everyone's prayers together with everyone else's and assigning the work of carrying to God the prayers made to all the varied saints who are patrons of this and that, of health and work and the soil and the sufferings of people.

I have prayed for what might harm me, and I have prayed that others might be harmed, or at least obstructed. I have wondered if those prayers were answered in ways I can't know.

The rain stopped at last and the water receded, leaving everything filthy and covered in mud. We returned to our beloved Timber Town, but we kids decided it ought to be called Mud Pie Town now. The church hadn't fallen into the river but it would take a Capital Campaign to raise the money to fix it. Father Michaels said we should pray that the Capital Campaign would succeed, though he knew that many, many people were badly off now because of the flood, and the bishop doubted the money could be raised. But by July the money had been raised and the men of the parish were volunteering to help fix the church.

August
It was the day before the Feast of the Assumption of the Virgin, which is a Holy Day of Obligation, which means you must go to

church just as if it were Sunday. There were extra confessions to go to on this afternoon, which I could now go to and had to do, if I wanted to go to Communion in the morning, which I did. In the pew I did my Examination of Conscience and I couldn't find anything except the time I told my brothers to shut up because I was doing my homework, which was a lie because I was just reading a book.

There was a line for confessions. Waiting in my pew I read my Instructions for a Good Confession. What is a sin? A cruelty to others; a false representation of ourselves; a failure to honor God and the Saints in all the times and places we can, in all the ways we can, as often as ever we can.

I had falsely represented myself to Thad and Willy and so I guess I had sinned. I hadn't been sure.

In the dark of the booth I confessed to Father Michaels. I asked him himself to forgive me, because the priest has the power to do that. *Father, forgive me for I have sinned.* When I was done with my one sin he spoke in Latin and blessed me (I could see the faint motion of his hand through the screen) and he told me to say a decade of the Rosary and he was shutting the grate when I said Father, can I ask you something? And he said Certainly.

Is it true that older people can't see their guardian angels and talk right to them and hear them?

He paused for a little and then said: They hear them in a different way. They see them in a different way.

But I knew from the little pause that it was a priest's way of saying Yes it is true. And he said: Our Lord tells us that faith is the evidence of things not seen, that what we believe but can't see has substance.

I said Oh. Thank you, Father. And he shut the grate.

I went to kneel in the pew in front of the Mary altar, where Mary is holding the baby and also holding out a rosary, which makes her look a little like a busy mom doing two things at once; but her face was as serene as always. I said my penance, the beads passing through my fingers as I murmured the prayers one by one, and with the saying of it my sin went away from me and my heart was cleansed. That's a nice feeling, your sin going away like dirty water down the drain. It would probably be a sin in itself to go out and sin just to feel that feeling. But I thought of it.

I went out of the church and sat on the steps and took my Brownie cap off (it was the only hat I could find that afternoon) and a group of nuns from the convent next to the church were going by together, their habits sweeping up the dry leaves that lay on the pavement. The beauty of them moving all together, the airs lifting their veils, their smiles and voices—they sang together, the younger ones, out of simple good cheer. I thought of being a nun, singing and never sinning again. Yet maybe the beauty of it was that it was something to see and not something to be, like geese you see in the autumn sky following the leader, all the same but each itself, and you want to join them. I *felt* I was among the nuns even though I wasn't, and wouldn't want to be, not really.

It's so nice, I said to my guardian angel. The voices. Singing.

It is, she said. It's the only way we angels ever talk to one another.

September

One night at dinner Dad told a joke. It was because of the new (or rather old) school bus that the parish had just got for the grade school, given to them by the Twin City Bible Camp because it was so broken down and shabby they wouldn't use it any more and had got another. The bus was needed to bring the children who lived out on the Timber Town road to Coalsburg to school and back again. It said Twin City Bible Camp on the side, but Sister Fausta the art teacher said she would get some yellow paint and paint that out and put St. John Bosco School on it. On Monday the priest was going to bless the bus.

The joke Dad told was this: A little public school had got a brand new bus, and wanted it to be blessed by the different clergy of the town. So the Protestant minister came and read some verses out of King James's Bible. And the priest came and said some Latin and dashed the bus with holy water. And then the rabbi came up and instead of any of that he cut two inches off the tailpipe.

My mother blushed and smacked my father's hand. But nobody would tell us why the joke was funny. I thought maybe it was just funny because rabbis do funny things.

When we got to school on Monday the side of the bus was painted and the new name lettered on very carefully. But it was really pretty old and battered. I looked at the tail pipe for no good reason and it was very rusty at the end and sort of decayed. After school was done Sister told us all to go out into the yard and those who were going to Timber Town road and Coalsburg should get on the bus and everyone else gather round. When we all got on and found a seat—there was a lot of arguing about that, and pretty soon Mr. Kowalski the groundskeeper, who was now going to be the bus driver too, got up and yelled that we should all pipe down—we could see that Father Paine was coming, and he was wearing his stole and his biretta and an altar boy came after him with the bucket of holy water and the thing the priest uses to sprinkle people and things with. Yes I know what they are really: the bucket is the *aspersorium* and the sprinkler is called the *aspergillum*. Robbie told me that and he is studying Latin and will maybe be a priest. He thought I would forget as soon as he told me but of course I didn't. I cannot ever be a priest.

Father Paine had a look of patient suffering, but he always does; it makes me think his name is the right name for him. He is so very kind and gentle and isn't suffering really, I don't think, any more than anybody. He crossed himself and said the *In nomine Domini* and we all did too, even we on the bus. And then the priest said *Aspergo te omnibus* and more and he splashed the water on us, and drops hit the windows and I thought of rain falling in the months of school still ahead even though this day was sunny and warm.

Then Mr. Kowalski started the bus, but it didn't start. It sort of shrieked or groaned, but nothing more. We all waited. He tried again, and this time the bus tried to start; it shook and made noise and then a loud bang came out the back and black smoke. Then it stopped. "It died," Mr. Kowalski called out the door to Father Paine. Father Paine thought a moment, and then he turned to the students and the nuns and the lunch lady and with his hands he told them to kneel. When they had knelt he crossed himself and prayed. We on the bus couldn't kneel but we folded our hands, except some boys. Mr. Kowalski turned the key again and the engine started. It was as if it didn't want to but it had to, like Dad getting up in the morning. The bus rocked and coughed and made small bangs out its rear end and a boy said a bad word about that and got shushed. Then as the priest stopped speaking and the people waited, the bus ceased to suffer, and began to breathe easy. The bad smoke smell went away and a good smell of September air came in the windows. The bus seemed to be happier, not so tense. And cleaner. It purred.

Father Paine smiled, and he waved to Mr. Kowalski to go ahead, and Mr. Kowalski very slowly moved the bus away from the school, as though he still wasn't sure it wanted to. But it picked up speed, and we all took a deep breath, and somebody laughed and somebody else cheered, and the bus was happy now. The seats seemed less stained and shabby, and the windows fit better in their frames. We turned onto the road that goes along by the school and then onto the road that goes along the river and then we couldn't any longer hear the kids and the nuns cheering from the lawn of the school beneath the pale statue of Our Lady. And after a time we on the bus were quiet and felt the shadows of leaves pass over us.

October

On the day of Hallowe'en Sister Rose of Lima, our principal, told us in school meeting to be careful how we dressed up that night. She reminded us that this night is the Eve of All Saints, and in the morning tomorrow we will go to church and honor all the saints, not only the ones we know but those many, many saints in heaven whose names are not known except to God and to those who have been visited by them, their families or their friends or their enemies. The night before the day of a great feast can be a risky time, she said, and this feast more than any other. We should be careful of how we dress up and what costumes and masks we pick, she said, because to dress up in costumes as ghosts or demons or figures of Death like skeletons or corpses might draw those very figures to walk with us. On this night they are allowed to walk abroad, and though the Church knows very well how they can be prevented from doing the harm they may wish to do, children out and about in the streets might not know that what seem to be other kids following them in costumes like theirs really aren't, and careless children can be threatened and their souls drawn out from the houses of their bodies unwitting and into the world to come.

A word to the wise is sufficient, Sister Rose of Lima said. She said this once every day more or less.

I was pretty safe because I wore a Brown Scapular (scapulars are sort of itchy and always get tangled around your neck but everyone puts up with that) and Our Lady of Mount Carmel has promised that no one who dies wearing it will die in a state of mortal sin. I had a Miraculous Medal as well, which my favorite teacher in first grade gave to me. Because of these things I wasn't afraid to walk in the night on All Hallows' Eve, at least not more than a little. But because of what Sister said I dressed up as Snow White.

Kids in my neighborhood of Timber Town would go to the houses in better neighborhoods, where you can knock on doors and say Trick or Treat and get better treats (not that I knew how to play tricks on anyone who gave me nothing). The way to get to those houses was to go up the street away from my neighborhood and cross the bridge over the old canal that runs to the river, which in the book has no name. I had heard—we all knew—that down under this bridge hoboes had their camp, and there were remains there of fires and cardboard shelters and tin cans. Kids told stories about the hoboes, that they could rob you or even kill you, but I didn't believe them; I said *I don't believe that story* but in that way you pooh-pooh stories you don't want to worry about. My brothers and their friends told the stories when we crossed the bridge, and they made claws of their hands and tried to be scary.

We knocked on the doors of the houses that had jack-o'-lanterns on their porches fearsome or silly, with their fiery smiles and eyes, and my bag was full of treats to bring home, and so we started back. Then the boys got the idea to run to the bridge and across and leave me alone on the street. That was very mean of them and stupid and I called after them and said I would tell when I got home. I was more angry than afraid, and I walked on toward the bridge in my Snow White dress as though nothing was amiss. I set out on the bridge over the hobo camp, where maybe once a child had been killed though probably not. I could see a kid ahead of me on the bridge, in a white sheet like a ghost. When I looked again he wasn't there, but I thought he wasn't actually gone. And then again he was there, but only sort of. He was dawdling, as though he wanted me to catch up with him and maybe be with him, and he'd take me with him as Sister Rose of Lima had said; but he didn't seem dangerous or evil to me, just lonely and sad. I spoke an Ejaculation under my breath: *Lord Jesus Christ have mercy on me and on all the living and the dead.* I felt the Miraculous Medal grow warm against my chest and I knew that I was safe. And after I got across the bridge I could no longer see the little ghost child. He had remained behind.

November

On the Feast of All Souls, the second day of November, I went to church after school to pray for the release of souls from their sufferings in Purgatory. On this day alone prayers of the living faithful can absolve them of their sins and admit them to heaven.

The church was pretty full and smelled of damp wool and candle smoke and people, a smell I always liked and didn't like at the same time. On the cards that were placed in every pew was printed the Prayer of St. Gertrude, in white script across a colored picture of a gravestone and a praying child. *Eternal Father, I offer Thee the Most Precious Blood of Thy Divine Son, Jesus, in union with the masses said throughout the world today, for all the holy souls in purgatory, for sinners everywhere, for sinners in the universal church, those in my own home and within my family. Amen.*

Sister Rose of Lima said that God had promised St. Gertrude that when her prayer was said on this day with a righteous heart, a thousand souls would be freed from their sufferings in Purgatory. I looked around me at the others gathered there also praying for the dead, and some of them wept, perhaps for someone once in their own home and within their family, and I thought of Cousin Winnie. I didn't know if it was allowed to pray for one soul in particular, but I thought of the kid I had seen on the bridge in the night and I asked in my prayer that if he was a soul in Purgatory he might be one among my thousand. I prayed also that if Cousin Winnie was in Purgatory he might be one too. And I said the prayer for the dead: *Eternal rest grant unto them, O Lord, and let perpetual light shine upon them.* I felt the rush of the thousands of escaping souls winging upward into perpetual light. I was happy and sad as well.

December

I wanted snow for Christmas very much. The last Christmas it had only rained, a small gray ceaseless rain that made the town's decorations look miserable and hopeless, like a birthday party no one has come to; and then the floods had come and turned Timber Town into Mud Pie Town. Empty buildings on Second Street along the river still had dark shadows showing where the river had risen to.

My guardian angel didn't know how to ask for snow on my behalf, because though there are saints to pray to for rain, and saints for fine weather, there aren't any saints to pray to for snow. But I thought I could get a hearing. That's what Dad would say when he went to talk to the union shop steward: I'll get a hearing. God will do what we ask, I knew, if we ask in the right way; but it's not always easy to know the right way.

I took down the Book of Saints from the shelf and started from the beginning, but there are a lot of saints (about twenty St. Johns) and it was hard to pay attention. In due time I found that there are certain saints who are called Ice Saints in far northern countries, where they need to know when cold weather will come. One was St. Servatus, and there was St. Agnes and St. Prisca, St. Mamertus and St. Boniface. If their feast days are cold it will stay cold a long time after. So maybe they could bring snow as well.

When Dad asked me what I was doing—making lists of saints' names, drawing charts and birthdates, writing prayers—I told him I was praying for snow. He said he didn't think God would answer such a prayer. Snow or no snow happens because of big weather patterns, which they show in the newspapers and describe in the short-wave radio broadcasts he liked to listen to. If God wanted to bring snow on a certain day—even His own Birthday—He'd have to start up the right weather patterns a long way back, long before you asked Him for snow. It can't just be Ta-da, here it is.

I said *If you abide in me, and my words abide in you, you shall ask whatever you will, and it shall be done unto you.* That's the Gospel of John. And Dad looked down at me sitting on the floor with the crayons and I knew he loved me even if he didn't think you could pray for snow and have your prayer answered.

No snow fell that week; the weather was cold but clear, day after day. I wore leather gaiters under my wool plaid skirt and watched the breath come from my mouth as though to tell me I was alive and warm inside; and I kept up my prayers to the Ice Saints.

On the Third Sunday of Advent Father Paine gave a sermon about prayer, and about asking for things in prayer. As though he knew about me and my plan. Dad looked at me beside him and winked.

What Father Paine wanted to explain to us was a question that he said many had. If God knows all that has befallen the world, and has known since before the beginning all that would befall the world, why should we pray that things will come out well for us and for everyone? Hasn't it all been decided already, the good and the bad?

And he said that time for God is different from the way it is for us, that to God everything that was or will be is happening in . . . well, you could say in one moment, but moments are parts of time, and there is no name for what God sees. And when God sees a thing that by chance the world in its progress is bringing about, and the thing doesn't conform to His will, He can easily reset the conditions in the past, even at the beginning of the universe, so that the thing won't happen after all: because there is no "after all" for God.

That is the power given by God to our Holy Church, and by delegation to each of us, Father Paine said, and his sad pained face was alight. If we petition Him correctly, and if what we ask doesn't conflict with His larger purposes, He can't refuse us. At each moment He can reform the whole history of the world again from its beginning so that it will come to be. We may ask what we will.

And we call those things miracles, and answered prayers, and sins.

I thought then, sitting with the others in the newly rebuilt church that still smelled sweetly of wood and tartly of plaster: It's like a movie.

It's like a movie, where you know that the good guys will win in the end, no matter how often they lose and lose, how much they suffer: you just know they'll win. And even so, through the movie you are afraid for them every minute, and cry out to them to watch for the bad guys sneaking up on them, and your heart races and you get tears in your eyes *just as though you didn't know*; but you do know.

And the reason is that those who wrote and made the movie know you want the good guys to win, and so do they; and whenever in the story they are writing it looks like they can't win the writers change the story of the movie so that in the nick of time it happens that they can, and they do. Just as we watching hoped and prayed they would.

When we went out of the church on that Third Sunday in Advent so long ago we found that it had begun softly to snow. By the end of the day it had worked up to a pretty good blizzard. That night with the wild flakes flying in the street lights and the sound of tire chains in the street I knelt beside my bed and said my prayers and gave thanks to St. Mamertus, St. Pancras, St. Servatus, St. Agnes, St. Boniface, and I seemed to see them high in the heavenly places, like great snowmen striding above Timber Town and Twin City and the high hills beyond, the snow falling like seed from their hands.

* * *

The boys and girls I knew in St. John Bosco School, and my brothers, and Sister Rose of Lima and Father Paine and Father Michaels and the mill workers and the men who helped to build the new church, all still live in Timber Town, and so do I. But in another way I left a long time ago. I lived in many places, and things happened to me that I could not even have known were possible in the world, and some of them were not good and were my fault and some of them were dreadful and the fault of many people or everyone; and yet even as I grew up I thought that whatever bad things happened, however we *stumbled* as Father Paine used to say, overall in the world things were getting better, and old bad things were going away. And it has grown harder and harder to think that way.

I knew, when I was a child and thought as a child, that in the world I lived in the good guys would win in the end even when it seemed impossible, because even if they went wrong and lost their way and made mistakes, God and His angels could always change the beginning of the world so that in some unexpected way it would come out right, even if it could only be made right after death; and because of what Father Paine said about time, I knew *how* God and His angels could change such things even though they couldn't know beforehand what wrong way the world would take, because we are God's creatures and we are endowed with free will. Because nothing is over in a book that's being written or in

God's world being made, not until everything is over and the book is finished and closed.

I still know now in the deepest part of me that it's so, and that all will be well, all will be well, all manner of thing will be well, no matter how long and sad and scary the story gets. I just wish that once again, just once more, I could believe that the ways of changing things are mine too, that I am a writer of the world: and that as we did in the Timber Town flood I could reach my hands into the world, into the story of our town and all our towns, and change things so that the good guys would not be defeated forever.

Totalitopia

But to return, if I may use the expression, to the future . . .
—J.B.S. Haldane, *Daedalus; or, Science and the Future* (1924)

1.

During a summer in the late 1960s I discovered an easy and certain method of predicting the future. Not my own future, the next turn of the card, or market conditions next month or next year, but the future of the world lying far ahead. It was quite simple. All that was needed was to take the reigning assumptions about what the future was likely to hold, and reverse them. Not modify, negate, or question, but reverse. It was self-evident that this was the right method, because so many of the guesses that the past had made about its then future—that is, my own present—had turned out to be not only wrong but the opposite of what came to be instead, the more so the farther ahead they had been projected.

You could, of course, riffle through the old predictions and now and then find some tool or technique, some usage or notion, some general idea of how things would get gradually better or suddenly worse, that seemed eerily to foreshadow the actual; but that was really a game, where you took some aspect of the *present* and tried to match it with what the past had once thought up. Captain Nemo's submarine is driven by a heatless inexhaustible power source—Jules Verne predicted the nuclear sub! What was never predicted correctly was what the present world would be *like*: like to be in and to experience. There is a wonderful moment in Edward Bellamy's influential futurist utopian tract *Looking Backward* (1889) where a character, having fallen asleep in the 1880s and awakened in the year 2000, rushes out of the house to see the new world—after fortunately finding among the hats on the hat rack by the door a hat that fits him. In the future we, at least we proper folk, will still not go "bareheaded" or "hatless" into the street, for fear of being thought mad or distracted.

So it seemed clear to me that if you simply reversed what the past had imagined, you got something close to the real existing present. The same principle would therefore work for the future, and I went about applying it to the limning of the world that would exist in, say, five hundred years' time. (I had nothing to do that summer. I had lost my job and was squatting in an unoccupied building as a sort of watchman. Marijuana had just been invented. It was the time and the moment to think up things never before thought up.)

What predictions could I reverse? One general assumption abroad at the time I set to work was that overpopulation would soon create a future of scarcity and desperate struggles for resources everywhere, including the rich First World, all earth filling with humans as with lemmings. So reverse that: perhaps as an unintended result of attempts to limit growth, numbers will cease to rise and start downward, and in the far future populations will be not large but small, maybe vanishingly small. Pollution, smog, river fires, acid rain spoiling the natural environment and making the built environment uninhabitable? No; smokestack industry, even all industry, will in time cease to grow, tumor-like and poisonous, and instead shrink away. The near-certain chance that eventually, by accident or on purpose, thermonuclear weapons would destroy even the possibility of civilization? No, no nuclear war—somehow it will be obviated. But if vastation by the Bomb were escaped, it looked certain that the peoples and nations would be knit ever more closely together by interlocking technologies, skiving off human differences and reducing us to robot cogs in a single ever-growing world machine; or, conversely, that technology would vastly increase wealth and scope for the fortunate in a groomed and gratifying One World with an opening to the stars. No, neither of those: no technology in the future, no space travel, even our current technology forgotten or voluntarily given up, becoming a wonderful dream of long ago, as we dream of knights in armor. So then, brutish neo-primitives squatting in the remains of a self-destroyed technoworld? No, no, that's what you'd *guess*, and it will therefore be different from that. Self-conscious mini-civilizations, I thought, highly cultivated yet without reading or writing, unknown to one another, with concerns we can't imagine, walking humbly on a wounded but living earth.

This vision was enthralling to me, convincing because so unforeseen: its roots in the present firm and deep yet so occult that they will only be able to be perceived after centuries. Above all it seemed to me to be a future that had no lesson for the present, gave no warning or hope, made no particular sense of history or the passage of time. Its unknowable origins lifted from the present the burden of needing to do the right thing *now* in order not to be punished in the time to come. There was no right thing that could be done; we would just have to do our best. The future would be strange, but all right.

Though I had not conceived it so, this pleasant obsession eventually generated a book, a novel, a science fiction, in which all the aeons-to-come details impossible to know were given form, though of course not the form they would or will really have. And when read now, forty years on, what is immediately evident about my future is that it could have been thought up at no time except the time in which I did think it up, and has gone away as that time has gone. No matter its contents, no matter how it is imagined, any future lies not ahead in the stream of time but at an angle to it, a right angle probably. When we have moved on down the stream, that future stays anchored to where it was produced, spinning out infinitely and perpendicularly from there. The process I engaged in is still viable, maybe, or as viable as it was then; but it must forever be redone. The future, as always, is now.

2.

My wife said to me, *The past is the new future.* She is given to remarks of that kind, full of vatic force yet requiring mental application on my part to make them useful. The sense I make of it is that instead of growing clearer as we probe it, the future has grown dimmer, less solid, almost hard to believe in, but the past has continued to expand rather than shrinking with distance: the actual things we did do have gained rather than losing complexity and interest, and the past seems rich, its lessons not simple or singular, a big landscape of human possibility, generative, inexhaustible.

As a guide to present action and long-term planning, the future is anyway relatively new. The shape of things to come was not a constant concern of most people for most of the past. The Romans could imagine future wars and the founding of new cities and dynasties, but these would resemble in most ways the old ones. Christians foresaw an absolute end to time and history located (depending on specific creed and perceived signs of the times) at varying distances from the present, but between now and then it was all to be much the same, only worse. The Founding Fathers announced a New Order of the Ages, but it was a new order that recalled or reinstated an older one, the old Republic of Virtue that existed in Rome or Athens. The idea of a future that will not at all resemble the past really only comes when advancing technology changes the conditions of life and work within a single generation. To that generation it is apparent that, just as the past differs radically from the present, so will the future.

At that point (it's not really a locatable point, and not a universal one, but it can be thought of as somewhere in the first half of the nineteenth century, earlier in some places, later in others) a change can also be discerned in the efforts of planners and projectors to determine the future shape of the coming world—"determine" both in the sense of finding out what it would be and in the sense of controlling it. Early utopias from Plato through Thomas More (inventor of the term) and on to Fourier were all about proper social organization, good laws, societies that fit human nature better than the state or society the utopian lived in. After this point utopias are almost all set not on remote islands or mountaintops but in the future, and all must take into account the force of accelerating technology on everything from wealth creation to population expansion to world peace. So also must all the dark warnings of decline, disaster, waste and failure that are the left hand of the predicting impulse. And both of these impulses, hope and fear, are swept up in, and give power to, the characteristic fictions of mass change and of futures that entirely replace pasts: books such as the one that my imaginings led me inevitably toward.

Science fiction shares methods and modes with other genres—boys' adventure, Gothic tale, fable, satirical allegory, philosophical romance—but from the beginning it gained extra-literary power from its prediction of actual marvels that were sure to come sooner or later. No other fiction, not even the tales of Darkest Africa or polar exploration, had that. The more often the future was imagined, however, and the more detailed the guesses, the more they proved unequal to the strange meanderings of real time. As the noted SF writer and poet Tom Disch made clear in his 1999 book *The Dreams Our Stuff Is Made Of: How Science Fiction Conquered the World*, the tropes developed in science fiction since 1900—alien invasions, telepathy, time travel, people-shaped robot helpers, travel to other planets, nuclear mutants, flying cars, immortality—are now universal in the culture without actually having come much closer in actuality, or even appearing at all. Meanwhile SF kept missing the things that in fact would happen. Disch's own best book, *334*, published in 1974 and predicting the world of 2025, entirely missed the digital age just then dawning—not computers, which everyone knew would rule the world, but the universal accessibility of them, our ever-present freedoms and enchainments. But then almost every writer did. By the time

William Gibson set his cyberpunk novels in a digital future, it had already come to be.

Today most serious science fiction—that is, the stories that put the genre to the most interesting and thoughtful uses—rarely presents itself as the bearer of news from the future, or seeks to acquire power from the act of prediction. (There are writers working in that realm which only genre writers call "mainstream" who are putting well-worn futures to use—Margaret Atwood, Cormac McCarthy, Jim Crace—while denying they have committed science fiction.) New work labeled SF is more likely to be set in an alternative present, a world wholly unlike this one and not having evolved from our past at all, the possibility of which is sometimes described as grounded in quantum mechanics and cosmology, or sometimes simply posited. Or it is transferred to a remade past, where now-obsolete technologies are presented as having been capable of weird developments that never happened: "steampunk" is the name for this variant. Or it becomes inseparable from fantasy, with vampires and gods and sorceries given the merest lick of pretend science or none at all. If it does dwell in possible futures, these are likely to be pervaded by a necessary irony, even parody: SF writers are well aware of the history of the future, and risk bathos if they are not.

"Who controls the past controls the future; who controls the present controls the past," George Orwell said in a well-known futurist novel. He didn't claim that who controls the past controls the present, but if we like to believe that strenuous efforts today will make a difference to the future that we, collectively, must one day suffer, then why not strive to imagine a past that would alter the present we live in? Why should the future be privileged as a realm of speculation? Thus the modern storytelling mode called "alternative history" or "the counterfactual," a mode that Philip Roth (who reads no fiction these days) seems to feel he invented in *The Plot Against America*. It's actually of course common, not to say ubiquitous: the idea that with only a tiny drift of events in one direction or another the present would not be as we see it; the Butterfly Effect of chaos theory, the law of unintended consequences, makes the present seem as unlikely, even marvelous, as any future. Darwin couldn't help but see evolution as a mode of one-way progress, no matter how he cautioned himself and us against it, but the more we study the earth's past the clearer it is that our present resulted from a continuous branching of long-past possibilities, a process describable neither as chance nor as necessity, going on forever, a process we perforce inhabit, facing both ways. It could have been different, and somehow still seems it might. The past is the new future.

3.

Given all this, it's unlikely that many writers would now be tempted to employ seriously the heuristic I developed and believed (probably wrongly) was original with me. But suppose that we—well, I—were to succumb to the temptation to apply it, see what might be descried in the dark forward and abysm of time. Science fiction may have ceded the future, but the imagineers are still busily working out what's certain to come, giving us fresh projections that might be reversed.

There is what the technophile and inventor Ray Kurzweil calls the Singularity, rapidly oncoming, in which human minds become powerfully knitted together as the wetware of the human person is integrated with the software and hardware of digital systems, thereafter evolving as one being, to who knows what heights or breadths. It's possible to point to current work wherein a wired person is able to move a cursor on a computer screen, just a little, by thought alone; it will get lots better than that, and at an accelerating pace.

But no, that's not happening. Will the mind be integrated with the machine? Yes it will, and already is, just as a hammer is integrated with a hand and able to do things neither is capable of by itself; but just as a hammer is not a hand, a machine is not a mind. Will we all exist together in a humming matrix of common culture and language, communicating so thoroughly and constantly that we will form a Hive Mind of undifferentiated permeable consciousness? No, or rather yes, just as in limited ways we are that now: there is no such thing as individual human consciousness existing without culture, without the minds and symbolic activities of others living and dead, and there never was or can be; but even so we are still, and will be still, individuals with consciousness. Increased digital capability will not in itself change our nature, no more (though perhaps no less) than did agriculture, steam, the telegraph, or printing; we will still recognize our old selves way back in nowadays, just as today we recognize ourselves in the Romans and the Six Nations. The idea that "social media" will wipe out a sense of history and submerge everyone in a froth of presentness is illusory. Even today anyone with a passing interest in the history of anything can learn far more than was wanted with a mouse-click or two, and scholars face data mountains that can take years to climb; I can't believe there will be less of it when mouse-clicks are as redolent of a simpler time as fountain pens are now.

The most unconscionable reversal of prophecy a new future must assert is the reversal of climate change, or at least a dramatic reduction such that it leaves humankind about where it was, *mutatis mutandis*. I suppose that like many of our public persons I could just assert that climate change isn't real, but that's cheating. I have no idea how we will survive it, but we will. (It's an oddity of futurist projects that most of them are actually backward-looking: a lot of their pages, and the author's efforts, are spent in accounting for how the imagined new state of things arose out of the one the reader is in. But I'm not writing a book.)

Another convincing future—I mean to those who have not adopted the Method—posits a general spread of liberal freedoms and open markets and moderate democracies, what Francis Fukuyama named (he has since modified the vision) the End of History. Recent events have been calling this pleasant future into question, however, strongly suggesting instead a continuation of the crimes, follies and misfortunes of mankind that Gibbon described as history's record. Authoritarianism, scarcity, and I'm-all-right-Jackism. Only the strong survive. Gated communities, unfree markets dominated by looters, politics by thugs and toadies. All this may obtain in the near future, though even that can be doubted, and the reverse of it will certainly develop (like a photograph from a negative) if we project far enough.

The one scenario *not* conceived of as remotely likely by any faction of futurians—the reverse really of all their competing auguries—is the possibility, and then the final achievement, of a generous and benevolent One World government, solving humankind's problems and adjudicating its disputes through the consent of the governed. The end of capitalism and its plutocrats and bought politicians. An antique among futures, that one, and impossible to envision on any grounds: political, economic, sociological, or simply the ground of basic human nature.

So that will be it. The future will consist of a new kind of universal anarcho-totalitarian system which is, on the whole, pretty successful at fostering human happiness and diversity as well as ensuring social justice and welfare. From each according to his abilities, to each according to his needs: Marx's formulation has always applied very well to individual families—it's how the best-run families function—but in future it will define the Family of Man. Kant's long-lost distinction between public and private, which is exactly opposite to the one in common use today, will then be universal: the *private* is the particular ethnic, religious, political, clan, or company loyalties we own; when we are *public* we engage the deepest human part of us, undifferentiated, possessed by all, recognizable in each.

A command economy, of course: that idea failed in the past because of lack of timely information and a disregard of personal desires, but the Internet 4.0, born out of the primitive workings of Google and Amazon, will fix that, and what you want—within reason—you can get. It seems impossible to us that, absent the Invisible Hand, entrepreneurial innovation can flourish, wants be met, and well-being increase—so it's clear that's what is to come.

These may sound like the commonest hopes (and doubts) we have had for technology, particularly information technology, for a century and more. But such hopes and doubts always foresee *plenty* as a consequence of the right worldwide deployment of powerful means, *rapidity* and *noise* as a function of interconnectedness, *manipulation* of fickle desires and dreads by Hidden Persuaders. No.

The future will show simplicity, asceticism (possibly as a result of scarcity: there may be enough for all, but not a lot more) and taking care, maybe too much care. Use it up, wear it out, make it do, do without. Certainly a democracy with as many parties as there are citizens, a parliament of all persons governing through a sort of fractal consensus which I cannot specify in detail, will spend a lot of time pondering. In fact it will be amazing (only to us imagining it now) how quiet a world it will be. A woman awakes in her house in Sitka to make tea, wake her family, and walk the beach (it runs differently from where it runs today). After meditation she enters into communication with the other syndics of a worldwide revolving presidium, awake early or up late in city communes or new-desert oases. Nightlong the avatars have clustered, the informations have been threshed: the continuous town meeting of the global village.

There is much to do.

4.

Any prediction about what is in fact to come, when cast as fiction, runs the risk not just of being wrong but of being not about the future at all. The two most famous futurist fictions of the 20th century—*1984* (which took place a mere thirty-odd years in the future) and *Brave New World* (set six hundred years on)—are of course best seen not as prediction but as critical allegories of the present. (They are like temporal versions of *Gulliver's Travels*, which could be called a geographical allegory.) That's why they still hold interest while more earnestly meant divinings don't. Both novels, which resemble each other closely while seeming to be opposites, are based on the if-this-goes-on premise—but this never does go on. Something else does. Both Orwell (if he had lived) and Huxley might have been tempted to congratulate themselves when the future seemed to trend away ever more sharply from their visions: their warnings had been heeded. Had they?

A third and less well-known novel—*We* by Yevgeny Zamyatin, 1921—certainly influenced Orwell, who claimed that it must certainly have influenced Huxley. Zamyatin invented a couple of the standard features of the future which would haunt science fiction from then on, including people with numbers rather than names and the possibly nonexistent but still omnipotent and omnipresent Leader. Its central trope is transparency: the whole numbered society, marching in unison, living in houses of glass, is bent on the creation of an enormous rocket ship aimed at the moon, also made entirely of glass. Like Orwell's and Huxley's it's a futurist novel that's not about the future. It differs from them in being not an allegory or an object lesson or warning of any kind but a transcendent personal vision, an impossibility rather than a possibility. Where Orwell's imagined world is shabby and cheap and nasty, and Huxley's brightly colored and silly, Zamyatin's is filled with an unsettling radiant joy, right through to its terrible ending. It has what Milan Kundera perceived in Dostoevsky's *The Idiot*: "the comical absence of the comical." Instead of perspicacity and authority, which in the predicting of the future are fatuous, there is beauty and strangeness, the qualities of art, which sees clearly and predicts nothing, at least on purpose. These are the qualities of all the greatest fictional representations of the future, books that, after the initial shock they carry has faded, can reappear not as tales about our shared future nor salutary warnings for the present they were written in but simply as works of disinterested passion, no more (and no less) a realistic rendering of this world or any world now or to come than is *The Tempest* or *The Four Zoas*.*

Time, W.H. Auden said, is intolerant and forgetful, but "worships language and forgives/Everyone by whom it lives." Time will leave my new and no doubt baselessly optimistic Totalitopia behind; it was being left behind even as I wrote it down. As prediction it might bewilder or bore, but as a work of art in language—if it were as easy to turn it into a work of art as it was to think it up—it might survive its vicissitudes in the turbulence of time and emerge sometime downstream as a valuable inheritance from the past, all its inadequate dreams and fears washed away. Meanwhile the real world then, no matter what, will be as racked with pain and insufficiency as any human world at any time. It just won't be racked by the same old pains and insufficiencies. It will be strange. It is forever unknowably strange, its strangeness not the strangeness of fiction or of any art or any guess but absolute. That's its nature. Of course holding the mirror up to nature is what Hamlet insisted all playing, or pretending, must do; but—as Lewis Carroll knew— the image in a mirror, however scary or amusing or enlightening, is always reversed.

---

* Among those, personal taste would select Disch's aforementioned *334*, Russell Hoban's post-atomic *Riddley Walker*, Cordwainer Smith's *Norstrilia* (14,000 years in the future!), J.G. Ballard's *Vermilion Sands*.

Everything That Rises

I HAVE COME TO perceive a cosmos filled with superintelligent beings—a virtually infinite number of them, whose minds have transcended their earthbound bodies and are independent of any particular substrate—a "connectome" thinking at fantastic speeds, light, effulgent, deathless. The beings are ourselves a thousand or ten thousand years in the future, networked across galactic distances and accompanied by every human consciousness that has ever existed, resurrected from the abysm of time by quantum recovery techniques that even now can be shown not to violate the laws of physics. And I have come to perceive how we on Earth now must begin the task of bringing this future about.

Actually, I don't perceive all this myself. But I spent a long day recently in the social-activities room of the New York Society for Ethical Culture, listening to the speakers at the Modern Cosmism conference describe these and other visions in PowerPoint presentations. Large color photographs on the walls showed galaxies and nebulae. The A/V system was a bit balky. There was boxed coffee. Close to a hundred people sat in stackable chairs, many of them familiar with the general concepts and eager to ask questions of the presenters. Several were of Russian origin, including Vlad Bowen, the conference's organizer and the executive director of the Cosmism Foundation. Over the course of the day the Russian cosmist tradition of past centuries was mentioned and honored as inspiration, but this conference was forward-looking to a high degree: the focus was on new cosmism, not old.

It's possible that without knowing much of anything about, say, theosophy, or naturism, or spiritualism, you could guess at their basic concepts and aims. But I doubt the same is true of Russian cosmism. The speakers at this conference were largely enthusiasts of cutting-edge science or sciencelike speculation, and their graphs and charts and videos described actual experimental results as well as far-off possibilities. Bowen opened the proceedings by describing the Greek concept of an original *chaos*—meaningless and formless—out of which arose a *cosmos,* ordered and beautiful. He noted, as once upon a time a classics teacher of mine had, that the words *cosmos* and *cosmetics* have the same root. But universal oneness and order is not what cosmists mostly contemplate now, and really it never was.

George Young, in his encyclopedic account *The Russian Cosmists,* calls the movement "oxymoronic": a blend of "activist speculation, futuristic traditionalism, religious science, exoteric esotericism, utopian pragmatism, idealistic materialism—higher magic partnered to higher mathematics." Many of the wildest speculators in the Russian tradition were scientists, including the physicist Nikolai Umov, the pioneering rocket theorist Konstantin Tsiolkovsky, and the geochemist Vladimir Vernadsky. Their grounding in science didn't hinder, and may have powered, their quasi-religious speculations, which most of them regarded as practical programs for long-term human action. Young argues that it's a specifically cosmist tendency to make every search for knowledge a starting point for work: to change every -*ology* into an -*urgy*. Thus theology yields theurgy: knowledge of God yields methods for putting God's power to work.

Nikolai Fedorovich Fedorov—a nineteenth-century librarian, philosopher, and secular saint—is still largely unheard-of outside Russia but a central figure in the history of Russian thought. He didn't use the term "cosmism," but his vast writings and, even more, his teaching and his friendships gave rise to the movement, as both theory and program, -*ology* and -*urgy*. For Fedorov, the central problem facing mankind (and he believed that indeed there is a central problem) was death, and the solution was to find the means and the will to defeat death, to make it powerless over the future and to rescue from its grasp everyone who has ever lived: a general resurrection of all the dead. We receive life from our mothers and fathers; our duty is to reverse the process and give life back to them. That is the "common task" he said was set for humanity.

This may sound like the most groundless kind of occult speculation, and it's true that cosmism was infused with esoteric Christian leanings. But Fedorov considered his immense project to be actually workable, achievable by as yet undiscovered technologies. To him death was disintegration, the disaggregation of the cells and molecules that compose us, which are subject to random scattering or lumping in lifeless concretions. To resurrect the dead would mean finding, separating, and reaggregating all the particles in the right order and with the right connections, whereupon they would return to life. Starting small—just one person reanimated, perhaps only briefly—the process would become more and more replicable, reach deeper into the past, and range further afield. The particles of the very earliest and longest dead have been carried away from Earth and into space as the world turns, but they must also be recovered and revived. For total resurrection we would have to reach the planets and even beyond to recover the "ancestral dust," to identify each person's contents, and (contra Humpty Dumpty) to put them together again. These journeys would have another benefit: by the time a fully resurrected population threatened to overwhelm old Earth, other planets would be ready to receive us. Fedorov thought that it would be possible to sail and steer Earth itself like a spaceship, out of its old orbit and on to who knows where.

For all of this extravagance, Fedorov fits into a long Russian tradition of extreme humility and selflessness. Though he corresponded with Tolstoy and intrigued Dostoevsky, he published little, and when his miscellaneous papers were collected and printed by his followers, he was dismayed. He gave away his exiguous salary as a Moscow librarian, did not buy clothes, never married, and hardly ate. (I can't bring myself to believe the repeated assertion that Fedorov didn't have a bed or blankets and for years slept on a humpbacked trunk. How is that possible? How did he not roll off every night, more than once? It seems like something in a fairy tale, in its own way as strange as the cosmic notions he and his devotees came up with.)

Fedorov's influence on, or at least his persistence in, later Russian thought has been long and queer, and could still be felt at the Modern Cosmism conference in far-off New York. The fact might have been noted—I don't think it was—that Fedorov's techniques of resurrection came to include the synthesizing or reengineering of bodies to be capable of living on many seemingly inhospitable planets, as well as the idea that a whole being could one day be resurrected from even a small trace of the former person. These ideas may only superficially resemble things like digitally uploaded minds and DNA, but the modern cosmists' impulses and aspirations really do reflect Fedorovian ones: transforming humans into posthumans, achieving immortality, leaving Earth, expanding experience.

You could argue that what distinguishes the modern cosmists is that they can report some actual progress in developing means and techniques to achieve those goals. True artificial intelligence and travel beyond the solar system are more than pure speculation; immortality via biological engineering can be thought of as an extension of current knowledge and practice. At least the World Transhumanist Association—whose symbol is a lovely graphic *h*+—thinks so. A little further off is the possibility of "substrate-independent minds." When I first heard the term I thought it meant minds unattached to any substrate, i.e., a ghost or spirit-self; but what's meant is cognition that arises from a substrate of any kind. In this view the mind is defined as the information state of the brain, and is immaterial only in the sense that the information content of a data file is. The brain is the substrate on which our information is stored and with which it is computed, but, the suggestion goes, it might be able to run on different hardware. Minds running on machine substrates can interface at speeds many times faster than our present abilities permit, and without error.

Cosmists old and new see human evolution as equivalent to progress, though evolutionary biologists mostly don't. Modern cosmists tend to be committed, not to say extreme, libertarian individualists, whereas the old cosmists dreamed of community and commonality. How do these visions comport? Through AI and IA ("intelligence augmentation"), people are becoming ever more linked. They are seeing and feeling the same things at the same moment around the globe, and though what spreads fastest among us right now seems to be various forms of spiritual and social infection, that may just be the growing pains of a future communitarian or libertarian utopia.

What if we really could upload our brains' information content—our "minds," in this formulation—into a machine substrate that would support the contents just as the brain does? Would it create a double of the original flesh-and-blood person? What would they say to each other? Which one of them could vote? Ben Goertzel, who appears everywhere in AI foundations, research groups, and affairs such as this conference (he has authored "A Cosmist Manifesto"), admitted that at present uploading would require the death of the original person. James Hughes, our conference transhumanist, suggested that if the self is an illusion, as Buddhists such as himself hold, then it can't matter what devices and instantiations the so-called self might pass through. But what if a digital person, while seeming to be conscious, claiming to be conscious, and passing all the possible tests to establish consciousness, really isn't—what if she is a "philosophical zombie," a mind without a person? How consciousness arises from the brain is of course unknown, and no digital substrate has yet been shown to be cognate in any practical sense to a biological brain, which remains the only substrate we know that actually does support minds and consciousness.

But what if you started from the other end, and created superior intelligences ab initio—artificial intelligence, minds that are "born digital"? Ben Goertzel predicts the appearance of an ultra-intelligent machine that would design better machines than people could. As Alan Turing's Bletchley Park collaborator I.J. Good long ago noted, the first ultraintelligent machine would be the last invention that people ever needed to make, bringing with it an inevitable "intelligence explosion." This is the much-talked-of (in these quarters at least) technological singularity, the point at which machines will create their own successors and incorporate all of us into their replications and thus their immortality.

So many ifs! Could quantum entanglement—the mysterious instant correlation of distantly separated subatomic particles—eventually make possible the connecting of every space-time moment to every other, and permit instant data channels between different places, different times, and different universes? If so, maybe "quantum archaeology" really could bring the dead back from when and where they are alive. Of course this would only allow the transmission of information, not stuff: Information You could cross time and space at the speed of light, but not the meat package that contains it, which by then will have been left behind anyway. At the conference, this vision was put before us by Giulio Prisco, a physicist and computer scientist, and a founding member of the wittily named Turing Church. (The Church–Turing hypothesis in mathematics defines what can be calculated by a "Turing machine," that is, a computer.)

I thought on the whole I'd prefer immortality to resurrection. (I have just reread that sentence and am astonished I could have typed it. If there are people who actually take sides on this issue, I was for a moment one among them.)

On reflection, the difficulty with the projects of modern cosmism and those of its allied societies, research groups, and churches (there is a Mormon Transhumanist Association) seems to me to be this: they begin with a premise that is far from proved, and then ponder the problems and possibilities that will follow if the premise is accepted. Sometimes our speakers seemed not to respect that "possible within the laws of physics" doesn't mean "practicable," much less "on its way to us now." Paradoxically, the old cosmist visions, despite their extravagance and insubstantiality, can seem richer and more immediate than modern cosmism's projects because they lack the drag of investment in actual, practical processes, which can seem primitive and doubtful, even wrongheaded. The connectome of our great benefactor *Drosophila melanogaster*, the endlessly studied common fruit fly, comprises some 135,000 neurons, plus associated synapses, and within years, not decades, it may be digitally replicated in its entirety. This may not produce an active Information Fruit Fly, because we really don't yet know how brains work, and simulation is not duplication. In any case, the human brain has nearly a hundred billion neurons, something like the number of stars in the Milky Way.

So what? Goertzel pointed out that the accepted physics has been overturned repeatedly through our brief human history and might well be again, and then again. As that great visionary Samuel Coleridge told himself in his diary:

> My dear fellow! never be ashamed of scheming—you
> can't think of living less than 4000 years, and that would

nearly suffice for your present schemes. To be sure, if they go on in the same ratio to the performance, then a small difficulty arises; but never mind! look at the bright side always and die in a dream!

After the final presentation there was wine in plastic cups and cubes of cheese and further talk. But I was weary and overloaded, and went up from the basement of the Society for Ethical Culture and out into the mild October evening. I turned south and in a couple of blocks came to Columbus Circle, which had been a rather sorry and worn-out place when I lived in New York, and was now a brilliant, glittering, magic city of its own, overtopped with a vast tower of glass and light that somehow gave the illusion of being no more than a meter thick. Crowds moved around the circle and the illuminated Columbus monument, extended minds connected by their phones and their earbuds and their speech in a dozen languages. They signaled with their sweatshirts, their shopping bags, their headscarves, and their faces. Crowds, because this was the weekend when Columbus and his explorations were celebrated: voyager who only dimly knew where he was going, and was wrong about where he arrived.

Gone

ELMERS AGAIN.

You waited in a sort of exasperated amusement for yours, thinking that if you had been missed last time yours would likely be among the households selected this time, though how that process of selection went on no one knew, you only knew that a new capsule had been detected entering the atmosphere (caught by one of the thousand spy satellites and listening-and-peering devices that had been trained on the big Mother Ship in orbit around the moon for the past year) and though the capsule had apparently burned up in the atmosphere, that's just what had happened the time before, and then elmers everywhere. You could hope that you'd be skipped or passed over—there were people who had been skipped last time when all around them neighbors and friends had been visited or afflicted, and who would appear now and then and be interviewed on the news, though having nothing, after all, to say, it was the rest of us who had the stories—but in any case you started looking out the windows, down the drive, listening for the doorbell to ring in the middle of the day.

Pat Poynton didn't need to look out the window of the kid's bedroom where she was changing the beds, the only window from which the front door could be seen, when her doorbell rang in the middle of the day. She could almost hear, subliminally, every second doorbell on Ponader Drive, every second doorbell in South Bend go off just at that moment. She thought: Here's mine.

They had come to be called elmers (or Elmers) all over this country at least after David Brinkley had told a story on a talk-show about how when they built the great World's Fair in New York in 1939, it was thought that people out in the country, people in places like Dubuque and Rapid City and South Bend, wouldn't think of making a trip East and paying five dollars to see all the wonders, that maybe the great show wasn't for the likes of them; and so the fair's promoters hired a bunch of people, ordinary-looking men with ordinary clothes wearing ordinary glasses and bow-ties, to fan out to places like Vincennes and Austin and Brattleboro and just talk it up. Pretend to be ordinary folks who had been to the fair, and hadn't been high-hatted, no sirree, had a wonderful time, the wife too, and b'gosh had Seen the Future and could tell you the sight was worth the five dollars they were asking, which wasn't so much since it included tickets to all the shows and lunch. And all these men, whatever their real names were, were all called Elmer by the promoters who sent them out.

Pat wondered what would happen if she just didn't open the door. Would it eventually go away? It surely wouldn't push its way in, mild and blobby as it was (from the upstairs window she could see that it was the same as the last ones) and that made her wonder how after all they had all got inside—as far as she knew there weren't many who had failed to get at least a hearing. Some chemical hypnotic maybe that they projected, calming fear. What Pat felt standing at the top of the stair and listening to the doorbell pressed again (timidly, she thought, tentatively, hopefully) was amused exasperation, just like everyone else's: a sort of oh-Christ-no with a burble of wonderment just below it, and even expectation: for who wouldn't be at least intrigued by the prospect of his, or her, own lawn-mower, snow-shoveller, hewer of wood and drawer of water, for as long as it lasted?

"Mow your lawn?" it said when Pat opened the door. "Take out trash? Mrs. Poynton?"

Now actually in its presence, looking at it through the screen door, Pat felt most strongly a new part of the elmer feeling: a giddy revulsion she had not expected. It was so not human. It seemed to have been constructed to resemble a human being by other sorts of beings who were not human and did not understand very well what would count as human with other humans. When it spoke its mouth moved (*mouth-hole must move when speech is produced*) but the sound seemed to come from somewhere else, or from nowhere.

"Wash your dishes? Mrs. Poynton?"

"No," she said, as citizens had been instructed to say. "Please go away. Thank you very much."

Of course the elmer didn't go away, only stood bobbing slightly on the doorstep like a foolish child whose White Rose salve or Girl Scout cookies haven't been bought.

"Thank you very much," it said, in tones like her own. "Chop wood? Draw water?"

"Well gee," Pat said, and, helplessly, smiled.

What everyone knew, besides the right response to give to the elmer, which everyone gave and almost no one was able to stick to, was that these weren't the creatures or beings from the Mother Ship itself up above (so big you could see it, pinhead sized, crossing the face of the affronted moon) but some kind of creation of theirs, sent down in advance. An artifact, the official word was; some sort of protein, it was guessed; some sort of chemical process at the heart of it or head of it, maybe a DNA-based computer or something equally outlandish, but no one knew because of the way the first wave of them, flawed maybe, fell apart so quickly, sinking and melting like the snowmen they sort of resembled after a week or two of mowing lawns and washing dishes and pestering people with their Good Will Ticket, shrivelling into a sort of dry flocked matter and then into nearly nothing at all, like cotton candy in the mouth.

"Good Will Ticket?" said the elmer at Pat Poynton's door, holding out to her a tablet of something not paper, on which was written or printed or anyway somehow indited a little message. Pat didn't read it, didn't need to, you had the message memorized by the time you opened your door to a second-wave elmer like Pat's. Sometimes lying in bed in the morning in the bad hour before the kids had to be got up for school Pat would repeat like a prayer the little message that everybody in the world it seemed was going to be presented with sooner or later:

GOOD WILL
YOU MARK BELOW.
ALL ALL RIGHT WITH LOVE AFTERWARDS
WHY NOT SAY YES
|__| YES

And no space for No, which meant—if it was a sort of vote (and experts and officials, though how such a thing could have been determined Pat didn't know, were guessing that's what it was) a vote to allow or to accept the arrival or descent of the Mother Ship and its unimaginable occupants or passengers—that you could only refuse to take it from the elmer: shaking your head firmly and saying No clearly but politely, because even *taking* a Good Will Ticket might be the equivalent of a Yes, and though what it would be a Yes *to* exactly no one knew, there was at least a groundswell of opinion in the think-tanks that it meant acceding to or at least not resisting World Domination.

You weren't, however, supposed to shoot your elmer. In places like Idaho and Siberia that's what they were doing, you heard, though a bullet or two didn't seem to make any difference to them, they went on pierced with holes like characters in the Dick Tracy comics of long ago, smiling shyly in at your windows, rake your leaves? Yard work? Pat Poynton was sure that Lloyd would not hesitate to shoot, would be pretty glad that at last something living or at least moving and a certified threat to freedom had at last got before him to be aimed at. In the hall-table drawer Pat still had Lloyd's 9mm Glock pistol, he had let her know he wanted to come get it but he wasn't getting back into this house, she'd use it on him herself if he got close enough.

Not really, no, she wouldn't. And yet.

"Wash windows?" the elmer now said.

"Windows," Pat said, feeling a little of the foolish self-consciousness people feel who are inveigled by comedians or MCs into having conversations with puppets, wary in the same way too, the joke very likely being on her. "You do windows?"

It only bobbed before her like a big water toy.

"Okay," she said, and her heart filled. "Okay come on in."

Amazing how graceful it really was; it seemed to navigate through the house and the furniture as though it were negatively charged to them, the way it drew close to the stove or the refrigerator and then was repelled gently away, avoiding collision. It seemed to be able to compact or compress itself too, make itself smaller in small spaces, grow again to full size in larger spaces.

Pat sat down on the couch in the family room, and watched. It just wasn't possible to do anything else but watch. Watch it take the handle of a bucket; watch it open the tops of bottles of cleansers, and seem to inhale their odors to identify them; take up the squeegee and cloth she found for it. The world, the universe, Pat thought (it was the thought almost everyone thought who was just then taking a slow seat on his or her davenport in his or her family room or in his or her vegetable garden or junkyard or wherever and watching a second-wave elmer get its bearings and get down to work): how big the world, the universe is, how strange; how lucky I am to have learned it, to be here now seeing this.

So the world's work, its odd jobs anyway, were getting done as the humans who usually did them sat and watched, all sharing the same feelings of gratitude and glee, and not only because of the chores being done: it was that wonder, that awe, a universal neap tide of common feeling such as had never been experienced before, not by this species, not anyway since the days on the old old veldt when every member of it could share the same joke, the same dawn, the same amazement. Pat Poynton, watching hers, didn't hear the beebeep of the school-bus horn.

Most days she started watching the wall-clock and her wristwatch alternately a good half-hour before the bus's horn could be expected to be heard, like an anxious sleeper who continually awakes to check his alarm clock to see how close it has come to going off. Her arrangement with the driver was that he wouldn't let her kids off before tooting. He promised. She hadn't explained why.

But today the sounding of the horn had sunk away deeply into her backbrain, maybe three minutes gone, when Pat at last reheard it or remembered having heard and not noticed it. She leapt to her feet, an awful certainty seizing her; she was out the door as fast as her heartbeat accelerated, and was coming down the front steps just in time to see down at the end of the block the kids disappearing into and slamming the door of Lloyd's classic Camaro (whose macho rumble Pat now realized she had also been hearing for some minutes.) The cherry-red muscle car, Lloyd's other and more beloved wife, blew exhaust from double pipes that stirred the gutter's leaves, and leapt forward as though kicked.

She shrieked and spun around, seeking help; there was no one in the street. Two steps at a time, maddened and still crying out, she went up the steps and into the house, tore at the pretty little Hitchcock phone table, the phone spilling in parts, the table's legs leaving the floor, its jaw dropping and the Glock 9mm nearly falling out: Pat caught it and was out the door with it and down the street calling out her ex-husband's full name, coupled with imprecations and obscenities her neighbors had never heard her utter before, but the Camaro was of course out of hearing and sight by then.

Gone. Gone gone gone. The world darkened and the sidewalk tilted up toward her as though to smack her face. She was on her knees, not knowing how she had got to them, also not knowing whether she would faint or vomit.

She did neither, and after a time got to her feet. How had this gun, heavy as a hammer, got in her hand? She went back in the house and restored it to the raped little table, and bent to put the phone, which was whimpering urgently, back together.

She couldn't call the police; he'd said—in the low soft voice he used when he wanted to sound implacable and dangerous and just barely controlled, eyes rifling threat at her—that if she got the police involved in his family he'd kill all of them. She didn't entirely believe it, didn't entirely believe anything he said, but he had said it. She didn't believe the whole Christian survivalist thing he was supposedly into, thought he would not probably take them to a cabin in the mountains to live off elk as he had threatened or promised, would probably get no farther than his mother's house with them.

Please Lord let it be so.

The elmer hovered grinning in her peripheral vision, like an accidental guest in a crisis, as she banged from room to room, getting her coat on and taking it off again, sitting to sob at the kitchen table, searching yelling for the cordless phone, where the hell had it been put this time. She called her mother, and wept. Then, heart thudding hard, she called his. One thing you didn't know, about elmers (Pat thought this while she waited for her mother-in-law's long cheery phone-machine message to get over) was whether they were like cleaning ladies and handymen, and you were obliged not to show your feelings around them; or whether you were allowed to let go, as with a pet. Abstract question, since she had already.

The machine beeped, and began recording her silence. After a time she punched the phone off without speaking.

* * *

Toward evening she got the car out at last and drove across town to Mishiwaka. Her mother-in-law's house was unlit, and there was no car in the garage. She watched a long time, till it was near dark, and came back. There ought to have been elmers everywhere, mowing lawns, taptapping with hammers, pulling wagonloads of kids. She saw none.

Her own was where she had left it. The windows gleamed as though coated with silver film.

"What?" she asked it. "You want something to do?" The elmer bounced a little in readiness, and put out its chest—so, Pat thought, to speak—and went on smiling. "Bring back my kids," she said. "Go find them and bring them back."

It seemed to hesitate, bobbing between setting off on the job it had been given and turning back to refuse or maybe to await further explanation; it showed Pat its three-fingered cartoon hands, fat and formless. You knew, about elmers, that they would not take vengeance for you, or right wrongs. People had asked, of course they had. People wanted angels, avenging angels; believed they deserved them. Pat too: she knew now that she wanted hers, wanted it right now.

She stared it down for a time, resentful; then she said forget it, sorry, just a joke sort of; there's nothing really to do, just forget it, nothing more to do. She went past it, stepping first to one side as it did too and then to the other side; when she got by she went into the bathroom and turned on the water in the sink full force, and after a moment did finally throw up, a wrenching heave that produced nothing but pale sputum.

Toward midnight she took a couple of pills and turned on the TV.

What she saw immediately was two spread-eagled skydivers circling each other in the middle of the air, their orange suits rippling sharply in the wind of their descent. They drifted closer together, put gloved hands on one another's shoulders. Earth lay far below them, like a map. The announcer said it wasn't known just what happened, or what grievances they had, and at that moment one clouted the other in the face. Then he was grabbed by the other. Then the first grabbed the second. Then they flipped over in the air, each with an arm around the other's neck in love or rage, their other arms arm-wrestling in the air, or dancing, each keeping the other from releasing his chute. The announcer said thousands on the ground watched in horror, and indeed now Pat heard them, an awful moan or shriek from a thousand people, a noise that sounded just like awed satisfaction, as the two skydivers—locked, the announcer said, in deadly combat—shot toward the ground. The helicopter camera lost them and the ground camera picked them up, like one being, four legs thrashing; it followed them almost to the ground, when people rose up suddenly before the lens and cut off the view: but the crowd screamed, and someone right next to the camera said *What the hell*.

Pat Poynton had already seen these moments, seen them a couple of times. They had broken into the soaps with them. She pressed the remote. Demonic black men wearing outsize clothing and black glasses threatened her, moving to a driving beat and stabbing their forefingers at her. She pressed again. Police on a city street, her own city she learned, drew a blanket over someone shot. The dark stain on the littered street. Pat thought of Lloyd. She thought she glimpsed an elmer on an errand far off down the street, bobbing around a corner.

Press again.

That soothing channel where Pat often watched press conferences or speeches, awaking sometimes from half-sleep to find the meeting over or a new one begun, the important people having left or not yet arrived, the backs of milling reporters and government people who talked together in low voices. Just now a senator with white hair and a face of exquisite sadness was speaking on the Senate floor. "I apologize to the gentleman," he said. "I wish to withdraw the word *snotty*. I should not have said it. What I meant by that word was: arrogant, unfeeling, self-regarding; supercilious; meanly relishing the discomfiture of your opponents and those hurt by your success. But I should not have said *snotty*. I withdraw *snotty*."

She pressed again, and the two skydivers again fell toward earth.

What's wrong with us? Pat Poynton thought.

She stood, black instrument in her hand, a wave of nausea seizing her again. What's wrong with us? She felt as though she were drowning in a tide of cold mud, unstoppable; she wanted not to be here any longer, here amid this. She knew she did not, hadn't ever, truly belonged here at all. Her being here was some kind of dreadful sickening mistake.

"Good Will Ticket?"

She turned to face the great thing, gray now in the TV's light. It held out the little plate or tablet to her. All all right with love afterward. There was no reason at all in the world not to.

"All right," she said. "All right."

It brought the ticket closer, held it up. It seemed to be not something it carried but a part of its flesh. She pressed her thumb against the square beside the YES. The little tablet yielded slightly to her pressure, like one of those nifty buttons on new appliances that feel, themselves, like flesh to press. Her vote registered, maybe.

The elmer didn't alter, or express satisfaction or gratitude, or express anything except the meaningless delight it had been expressing, if that's the word, from the start. Pat sat again on the couch, and turned off the television. She pulled the afghan (his mother had made it) from the back of the couch and wrapped herself in it. She felt the calm euphoria of having done something irrevocable, though what exactly she had done she didn't know. She slept there a while, the pills having grown importunate in her bloodstream at last; lay in the constant streetlight that tiger-striped the room, watched over by the unstilled elmer till gray dawn broke.

* * *

In her choice, in the suddenness of it, what could almost be described as the insouciance of it if it had not been experienced as so urgent, Pat Poynton was not unique or even unusual; worldwide, polls showed, voting was running high against life on earth as we know it, and in favor of whatever it was that your YES was said to, about which opinions differed. The alecks of TV smart and otherwise detailed the rising numbers, and an agreement seemed to have been reached among them all, an agreement shared in by government officials and the writers of newspaper editorials, to describe this craven unwillingness to resist as a sign of decay, social sickness, repellently non-human behavior: the newspeople reported the trend toward mute surrender and knuckling under with the same faces they used for the relaying of stories about women who drowned their children or men who shot their wives to please their lovers, or of snipers in faraway places who brought down old women out gathering firewood: and yet what was actually funny to see (funny to Pat and those like her who had already felt the motion of the soul, the bone-weariness too, that made the choice so obvious) was that in their smooth tanned faces was another look never before seen there, seen before only on the faces of the rest of us, in our own faces: a look for which Pat Poynton anyway had no name but knew very well, a kind of stricken longing: like, she thought, the bewildered look you see in kids' faces when they come to you for help.

It was true that a certain disruption of the world's work was becoming evident, a noticeable trend toward giving up, leaving the wheel, dropping the ball. People spent less time getting to the job, more time looking upward. But just as many now felt themselves more able to buckle down, by that principle according to which you get to work and clean your house before the cleaning lady comes. The elmers had been sent, surely, to show us that peace and cooperation were better than fighting and selfishness and letting the chores pile up for others to do.

For soon they were gone again. Pat Poynton's began to grow a little listless almost as soon as she had signed or marked or accepted her Good Will Ticket, and by evening next day, though it had by then completed a list of jobs Pat had long since compiled but in her heart had never believed she would get around to, it had slowed distinctly. It went on smiling and nodding, like an old person in the grip of dementia, even as it began dropping tools and bumping into walls, and finally Pat, unwilling to witness its dissolution and not believing she was obliged to, explained (in the somewhat overdistinct way we speak to not real bright teenage babysitters or newly hired help who have just arrived from elsewhere and don't speak good English) that she had to go out and pick up a few things and would be back soon; and then she drove aimlessly out of town and up toward Michigan for a couple of hours.

Found herself standing at length on the dunes overlooking the lake, the dunes where on a summer night she and Lloyd had first. Though he had not been the only one, only the last of a series that seemed for a moment both long and sad. Chumps. Herself too, fooled bad, and not just once or twice either.

Far off, where the shore of the silver water curved, she could see a band of dark firs, the northern mountains rising. Where he had gone or threatened to go. Lloyd had been part of a successful class-action suit against the company where he'd worked and where everybody had come down with Sick Building Syndrome, Lloyd being pissed off enough (though not ever really deeply affected as far as Pat could ever tell) to hold out with a rump group for a higher settlement, which they got, too; that was what got him the classic Camaro and the twenty acres of high woods. And lots of time to think.

Bring them back, you bastard, she thought; at the same time thinking that it was her, that she should not have done what she did, or should have done what she did not do; that she loved her kids too much, or not enough.

They would bring her kids back; she had become very sure of that, fighting down every rational impulse to question it. She had voted for an inconceivable future, but she had voted for it for only one reason: it would contain—had to contain—everything she had lost. Everything she wanted. That's what the elmers stood for.

She came back at nightfall, and found the weird deflated spill of it strung out through the hallway and (why?) halfway down the stairs to the rec room, like the aftermath of a foam fire-extinguisher accident, smelling (Pat thought, others described it differently) like buttered toast; and she called the 800 number we all had memorized.

And then nothing. There were no more of them, if you had been missed you now waited in vain for the experience that had happened to nearly everyone else, uncertain why you had been excluded but able to claim that you, at least, would not have succumbed to their blandishments; and soon after it became apparent that there would be no more, no matter how well they had been received, because the Mother Ship or whatever exactly it was that was surely their origin also went away: not *away* in any trackable or pursuable direction, just away, becoming less distinct on the various tracking and spying devices, producing less data, fibrillating, becoming see-through finally and then unable to be seen. Gone. Gone gone gone.

And what then had we all acceded to, what had we betrayed ourselves and our leadership for, abandoning all our daily allegiances and our commitments so carelessly? Around the world we were asking that, the kind of question that results in those forlorn religions of the abandoned and forgotten, of those who have been expecting big divine things any moment and then find out they are going to get nothing but a long, maybe a more than life-long, wait and a blank sky overhead. If their goal had been to make us just dissatisfied, restless, unable to do anything at all but wait to see what would now become of us, then perhaps they had succeeded; but Pat Poynton was certain they had made a promise, and would keep it: the universe was not so strange, so unlikely, that such a visitation could occur, and come to nothing. Like many others she lay awake looking up into the night sky (so to speak, up into the ceiling of her bedroom in her house on Ponader Drive, above or beyond which the night sky lay) and said over to herself the little text she had assented or agreed to: *Good will. You sign below. All all right with love afterwards. Why not say yes?*

At length she got up, and belted her robe around her; she went down the stairs (the house so quiet, it had been quiet with the kids and Lloyd asleep in their beds when she had used to get up at five and make instant coffee and wash and dress to get to work but this was quieter) and put her parka on over her robe; she went out barefoot into the back yard.

Not night any longer but a clear October dawn, so clear the sky looked faintly green, and the air perfectly still: the leaves falling nonetheless around her, letting go one by one, two by two, after hanging on till now.

God how beautiful, more beautiful somehow than it had been before she decided she didn't belong here; maybe she had been too busy trying to belong here to notice.

All all right with love afterwards. When though did afterwards start? When?

There came to her as she stood there a strange noise, far off and high up, a noise that she thought sounded like the barking of some dog-pack, or maybe the crying of children let out from school, except that it wasn't either of those things; for a moment she let herself believe (this was the kind of mood a lot of people were understandably in) that this was it, the inrush or onrush of whatever it was that had been promised. Then out of the north a sort of smudge or spreading dark ripple came over the sky, and Pat saw that overhead a big flock of geese were passing, and the cries were theirs, though seeming too loud and coming from somewhere else or from everywhere.

Going south. A great ragged V spread out over half the sky.

"Long way," she said aloud, envying them their flight, their escape; and thinking then No they were not escaping, not from earth, they were of earth, born and raised, would die here, were just doing their duty, calling out maybe to keep their spirits up. Of earth as she was.

She got it then, as they passed overhead, a gift somehow of their passage, though how she could never trace afterwards, only that whenever she thought of it she would think also of those geese, those cries, of encouragement or joy or whatever they were. She got it: in pressing her Good Will Ticket (she could see it in her mind, in the poor dead elmer's hand) she had not acceded or given in to something, not capitulated or surrendered, none of us had though we thought so and even hoped so: no she had made a promise.

"Well yes," she said, a sort of plain light going on in her back-brain, in many another too just then in many places, so many that it might have looked—to someone or something able to perceive it, someone looking down on us and our earth from far above and yet able to perceive each of us one by one—like lights coming on across a darkened land, or like the bright pinpricks that mark the growing numbers of Our Outlets on a TV map, but that were actually our brains, *getting it* one by one, brightening momentarily, as the edge of dawn swept westward.

They had not made a promise, *she* had: good will. She had said yes. And if she kept that promise it would all be all right, with love, afterwards: as right as it could be.

"Yes," she said again, and she raised her eyes to the sky, so vacant, more vacant now than before. Not a betrayal but a promise; not a letting-go but a taking-hold. Good only for as long as we, all alone here, kept it. All all right with love afterwards.

Why had they come, why had they gone to such effort, to tell us that, when we knew it all along? Who cared that much, to come to tell us? Would they come back, ever, to see how we'd done?

She went back inside, the dew icy on her feet. For a long time she stood in the kitchen (the door unshut behind her) and then went to the phone.

He answered on the second ring. He said hello. All the unshed tears of the last weeks, of her whole life probably, rose up in one awful bolus in her throat; she wouldn't weep though, no not yet.

"Lloyd," she said. "Lloyd, listen. We have to talk."

In the Tom Mix Museum

1958, AND WE ARE going to the Museum of Tom Mix. It is in a place called Dewey. "Dewy" is what my father calls my sister. A dewy girl. She lowers her eyes to not see him looking at her. I have my guns on, I buckle them on every morning when I put on my jeans. They have ivory handles with rearing horses carved on them that look like Tony, Tom Mix's horse. My father's name is Tony too. There is a horse on the hood of the car, and my father said we follow the horse wherever it goes. I used to watch for the horse to turn right or left, to see if the car went that way, and every time it did. But I am older now and I get it. Tony was a trick pony. My mother says that my father is a one-trick pony. Tony can think and talk almost like a person (Tony the horse).

The Museum of Tom Mix *is* Tom Mix, but Tom Mix is much larger than you would think, taller than the statue of Paul Bunyan in that other town. We go around to the back of his left boot, which has a heel as high as I am, with a door in it. We go in one by one. There is a stairway up to the top of Tom Mix, and it is dark at the top. Tony is there, halfway up; then above Tony is the other Tony, after Tony died, and above him another. Far, far up are Tom Mix's narrowed eyes, letting in the light. We are standing together, I love them all, and we wait to see who will start to climb.

And Go Like This

There is room enough indoors in New York City for the whole 1963 world's population to enter, with room enough inside for all hands to dance the twist in average nightclub proximity.
—Buckminster Fuller

DAY AND NIGHT THE jetliners come in to Idlewild fully packed, and fly out again empty. Then the arrivals have to get into the city from the airports—special trains and buses have been laid on, of course, day and night crossing into the city limits and returning, empty bean cans whose beans have been poured out, but the waits are long. The army of organizers and dispatchers, who have been recruited from around the world for this job—selfless, patient as saints, minds like adding machines, yet still liable to fainting fits or outbursts of rage, God bless them, only human after all—meet and meet and sort and sort the incomers into neighborhoods, into streets in those neighborhoods, addresses, floors, rooms. They have huge atlases and records supplied by the city government, exploded plans of every building. They pencil each room and then mark it in red when fully occupied.

Still there are far too many arriving to be funneled into town by that process, and thousands, maybe tens of thousands finally, set out walking from the airport. It's easy enough to see which way to go. Especially people are walking who walk anyway in their home places, bare or sandaled feet on dusty roads, with children in colorful slings at their breasts or bundles on their heads—those are the pictures you see in the special editions of *Life* and *Look*, tall Watusis and small people from Indochina and Peru. Just walking, and the sunset towers they go toward. How beautiful they are, patient, unsmiling, in their native dress, the Family of Man.

We have set out walking too, but from the west. We've calculated how long it will take from our home and we've decided that it can't take longer than the endless waits for trains and planes and buses, to say nothing of the trip by car. No matter how often we've all been warned not to do it, *forbidden* to do it (but who can turn them back once they've set out?) people have been piling into their station wagons and sedans, loading the trunk with coolers full of sandwiches and pop, a couple of extra jerry-cans of gas— about a dollar a gallon most places!—and setting out as though on some happy expedition to the National Parks. Now those millions are coming to a halt, from New Jersey north as far as Albany and south to Philadelphia, a solid mass of them, like the white particles of precipitate forming in the beaker in chemistry class, drifting downward to solidify. Then you have to get out and walk anyway, the sandwiches long gone and the trucks with food and water far between.

No, we've left the Valiant in the carport and we're walking, just our knapsacks and identification, living off the land and the kindness of strangers.

* * *

There was a story in my childhood, a paradox or a joke, which went like this: Suppose all the Chinamen have been ordered to commit suicide by jumping off a particular cliff into the sea. They are to line up single file and each take his or her turn, every man woman and child jumping off, one after the other. And the joke was that the line would never end. For the jumping-off of so many would take so long, even at a minute a person, that at the back of the line lives would have to led by those waiting their turn, and children would be born, and more children, and children of those children even, so that the line would go on and people would keep jumping forever.

This, no, this wouldn't take forever. There was an end and a terminus and a conclusion, there was a finite number to accommodate in a finite space—that was the *point*—though of course there would be additions to the number of us along the way, that was understood and accounted for, the hospital spaces of the city have been specially set aside for mothers-to-be nearing term, and anyway how much additional space can a tiny newborn use up? In those hospitals too are the old and the sick and yes the dying, it's appalling how many will die in this city in this time, the entire mortality of earth, a number not larger than in any comparable period of course, maybe less for that matter, because this city has some of the best medical care on earth and doctors and nurses *from around the world* have also been assigned to spaces in clinics, hospitals, asylums, overwhelmed as they might be looking over the sea of incapacity, as though every patient who ever suffered there has been resurrected and brought back, hollow-eyed, gasping, unable to ambulate.

But they are there! That's what we're not to forget, they are all there with us, taking up their allotted spaces—or maybe a little more, because of having to lie down, but never mind, they'll all be back home soon enough, they need to hang on just a little longer. And every one who passes away before the termination, the all-clear, whatever it's to be called, will be replaced, very likely, by a newborn in the ward next door.

And what about the great ones of the world, the leaders and the Presidents for Life and the Field Marshals and the Members of Parliaments and Presidiums, have they really all come? If they have, we haven't been informed of it—of course there are some coming with their nations, but the chance of being swallowed up amid their subjects or constituents, suffering who knows what indignities and maybe worse, has perhaps pushed a lot of them to slip into the city unobserved on special flights of unmarked helicopters and so on, to be put up at their embassies or at the Plaza or the Americana or in the vast apartments of bankers and arms dealers on Park Avenue. Surely they have left behind cohorts of devoted followers, henchmen, whatever, men who can keep their fingers on the red button or their eyes on the skies, just in case it has all been a trap, but we have to be realistic: not every goat-herd in Macedonia, every bushman in the Kalahari is going to be rounded up, and they don't need to be for this to work—you can call your floor thoroughly swept even if a few twists of dust persist under the couch, a lost button beneath the radiator. *The perfect is the enemy of the good.* He's an engineer, he must know that.

And it *is* working. They are filling, from top to bottom, all the great buildings, the Graybar Building, the Pan Am Building, Cyanamid, American Metal Climax, the Empire State—a crowd of Dutch men and women and children fill the souvenir shop at the top of the Empire State Building, milling, handling the small models, glass, metal, plastic, of the building they are in. The Metropolitan Museum is filling as though for a smash hit opening, Van Gogh, Rembrandt, the Modern as for a Pollack retrospective or Op Art show, there is even champagne! How is it that certain people have managed to gather with people like themselves, as on Fifth Avenue, at the Diocesan headquarters, Scribner's bookshop, the University Club, whereas old St. Patrick's is crowded with just everybodies, as though they had all come together to pray for rain in a drought, or to be safe from an invading army? They *are* the invading army!

We know so little, really, plodding along footsore and amazed yet strangely elated among the millions, the *river of humanity*, as Ed Sullivan said in his last column in the *Daily News* before publishing was suspended for the duration. The broad streets (Broadway!) just filled all the way across with persons, a river breaking against the fronts of the dispatcher stations, streams diverted, uptown, which is north more or less, downtown, which is south. And now the flood is at last beginning to lessen, to loosen, a vortex draining away into the shops and the apartments, the theaters and the restaurants.

* * *

She and I have received our assignment. The building is in Manhattan, below Houston Street, which we have learned divides the newer parts of the city from the older parts. Though old Greenwich Village is mostly above it and all of Wall Street is below it. We would like to have been ushered down that far, to find a space for ourselves in one of those titans of steel and glass, where perhaps we could look out at the Statue of Liberty and the emptied world. We were surprised to find we both wished for that! I'd have thought she'd want a small brownstone townhouse on a shady street. Anyway it's neither of those, it's a little loft on the corner of Spring Street and Lafayette Street, an old triangular building just five stories tall. Looking down on us from the windows on the east side of the street as we walk that way are Italian men and women, not people just arrived from Italy but the families who live in those places, for that's Little Italy there, and the plump women in housedresses, black hair severely pulled back, and the young men with razor-cut hair and big wristwatches are the tenants there. They're waving and shouting comments down to the crowd endlessly passing, friendly comments or maybe not so friendly, hostile even maybe, their turf invaded, not the right attitude for now.

But here we are, number 370, we wait our turn to go in and up. Stairs to the third floor. It seems artists now live in the building, they are allowed to, painters, we smell linseed oil and canvas sizing. Our artist is lean, scrawny almost, his space nearly empty, canvases leaning against the wall, their faces turned away. We look down— maybe shy—and can see in the cracks of the old floorboards what she says are *metal snaps*, snaps for clothing, from the days when clothes were made here by immigrants. Our artist is either happy to see us or not happy, excited and irritated, that's probably universal, we are all cautious about saying anything much to him or to one another, after all *he* didn't invite us. *Okay, okay* he keeps saying. Is that dark brooding resentful girl in the black leotard and Capezios his girlfriend?

Well, better here than in some vast factory floor in the borough of Queens or train shed in Long Island City, or out on Staten Island, not much different from where we come from. The ferries are leaving from Manhattan's tip for Staten Island every few minutes, packed with people to the gunwales or the scuppers or whatever those outside edges are called. World's cheapest ocean voyage, they say, just a nickel to cross the white-capped bay; Lady Liberty, Ellis Island deserted and derelict over that way, where once before the millions came into New York City to be processed and checked and sent out into the streets. The teeming streets. *I lift my lamp beside the golden door.* For a moment, thinking of that, looking down at those little metal snaps that slipped from women's fingers fifty, sixty years ago, it all seems to make sense, a human experiment, a *proof* of something finally and deeply good about us and about this city, though we don't know what, not exactly.

It's the last day, the last evening: we're lucky to have arrived so late, there won't be problems with food supplies or sleeping arrangements that others are having. The plan has worked so smoothly! All the populations are being accommodated, there are fights and resistance reported in various locations, but these are being handled by the large corps of specially trained minimally armed persons—*not* police, not soldiers, for the police forces and the armies were the first to arrive and be distributed, for obvious reasons—because they could be ordered to, and because of what they might do if left behind till last. And now it's done: everywhere, in every land, palm and pine, the planners and directors and their staffs have taken off their headsets, shut down their huge computers and telephone banks and telex machines—a worldwide web of information tools whose only goal has been this, this night. They have boarded the last 707s to leave Bombay, Leningrad, Johannesburg, and been taken just like all the others to the airports in New Jersey and Long Island, and when they have deplaned the crews too leave the airplanes parked and take the last buses into the city, checking their assignments with one another, joking—pilots and stewies, they're used to bunking in strange cities. When the buses have been emptied the drivers turn them off and leave them in the streets, head for the distribution centers for assignments. Last of all the dispatchers, all done: they can hardly believe it, not an hour's sleep in twenty-four, their ad hoc areas littered with coffee cups, telexes, phone slips, fanfold paper, cartons from the last Chinese restaurants: they gather themselves and go out into the bright streets—the grid is holding!—and they take themselves to wherever they have assigned themselves, not far because they're walking, all the trains and taxis have stopped, no one left to ride or drive them; they mount the stairs or take the elevators up to where they are to go.

It's done. The streets now empty and silent. *The city holds its breath*, they will say later.

In our loft space we have been given our drinks and our canapés. It's not silent here: we allow ourselves to joke about it, about our being here, we demand fancy cocktails or a floor show, but in a just-kidding way—actually it's strangely hard to mingle. She and I stick together, but we often do that at parties. We stand at the windows; we think they look toward the southeast, in the direction of most of the world's population, though we can't see anything, not even the night sky. Every window everywhere is lit.

But think of the darkness now over all the nightside of earth. The *primeval* darkness. For all the lights out there have been turned off, or not turned on, perhaps not *all* but so many. The quiet of all that world, around the earth and back again almost to here where we stand, this little group of islands, these buildings alight and humming, you can almost hear the murmur and the milling of the people.

He was right. It could be done, he knew it could be and it has been, we've done it. There's a kind of giddy pride. Overpopulation is a myth! There are so few of us compared to Spaceship Earth's vastness, we can feel it now for certain in our hearts, we hear it with our senses.

But—many, many others must just now be thinking it too—there's more. For now the whole process must be reversed, and they, we, have to go home again. To our home places, spacious or crowded. And won't we all remember this, won't we think of how for a moment we were all together, so close, a brief walk or a taxi ride all that separates any one of us from any other? And won't that change us, in ways we can't predict?

Did he expect that, did he think of it? Did he *know* it would happen? Moon-faced little man in his black horn-rims, had he known this from the start?

One final test, one final proof only remains. We've received our second drink. At the turntable our host places the 45 on the spindle and lets it drop. In every space in the city just at this moment, the same: on every record player, over every loudspeaker. The needle rasps in the groove—maybe there's a universal silence for a moment, an *expectant* silence, maybe not—and then the startlement of music. That voice crying out, strangely urgent, almost pleading, to take his little hand, and go like this.

Alone together in the quiet world, the nations begin to twist.

Paul Park's Hidden Worlds

THERE ARE WRITERS WHOSE biographies—in the sense of the life-stories they tell themselves about themselves—are an important force in their work, and writers whose private lives are largely irrelevant to what they write. Probably no writer can write entirely beyond the pressure of his or her own life, but those writers whose work couldn't exist without the basis of their life experiences are identifiable: Joyce, Woolf, D.H. Lawrence, Malcolm Lowry, many others, more of them the nearer we come to the present. But the writers of works now generally classed as "genre"—thrillers, horror novels, fantasy and science fiction, mysteries—seem the ones who put their lives to the least use. (New trends in mysteries, especially those from up above the 50th parallel, break away from this in certain ways.) The reason of course is that worlds created in such work have to function in ways that ordinary life-courses don't fit into, and writers who attempt to insert their own conflicted and unsummable selves within the constraints of planetary romance or international spy chases or alternate-universe battles risk bathos.

Paul Park's new collection *Other Stories* complicates these truisms in interesting ways. Park is not a realist or "mimetic" novelist.

His first science fiction/fantasy series began to appear in 1984; he has written other-planet SF and a historical fantasia about Jesus. For much of the past decade he has been creating a four-volume epic set in a reimagined *fin-de-siècle* Europe charged with magic and dream. But his shorter work is infused with fragments and perspectives drawn from his own and his family's life. Some of the stories are frank about the intersection of his life and times with other times and realms, others are more sideways, but none are directly autobiographical or naturalistic. *Other Stories* includes several of these, and the brief afterwords Park has added to each story make the connections apparent, or at least conjure them up. Several raise the question of whether in order for the fiction to have its full effect the biographical material has to be known—if the man himself, even, has to be known.

In an interview with the SF journal *Locus*, Park described how these metafictions arose: "A lot of things happen in my fiction through a process of accumulation rather than design," he reports. "For example, I had loose characters wandering around in my stories and I hadn't named them yet, so I gave them the name Paul Park as a placeholder. For me, naming characters is almost the most artificial thing you do in fiction. You have a character and you think, 'Is this Joe Doakes? Is this Francesco Bellesandro? Who is this?' At a certain point I just called a lot of them Paul Park. . . . When I started to publish those stories it was natural for people to make some connection between the character and the author because we had the same name." Well, yes. He then came to see how interest could arise when readers came to believe that they could see traces of a real life—of his, Paul Park's real life—even in genre or "extremely mannered" fiction.

Whether this is actually how the several stories that bear on this notion in *Other Stories* came to be as they are, or if the explanation is itself a metafictional dodge, is a question to be addressed. But to arrive at that I'll look at Park's earlier work, which to me forms a major achievement not only in the standard bookstore/publisher genres—to which it does truly belong—but in the larger or general realm of fiction as well.

His first three novels formed a trilogy, the Starbridge Chronicles, set in a world where seasons take tens of thousands of days to pass, and where a pervasive and death-oriented religion supports a vast militarized power structure. There is an Earth, and other planets, but not ours; there is an ancient hereditary monarchy, great castles, mounted soldiers, but also photographs, pickup trucks, cardboard boxes, gallows, cigars, perfumes, automatic rifles, monkish orders. The three books—their marvelous titles are *Soldiers of Paradise*, *Sugar Rain*, and *The Cult of Loving Kindness*—don't have the simple forward drive of fantasy epics deriving from Tolkien (and Tolkien's forebears), nor the sort of endpoint to which stories like those aim. There are dozens of characters, and none is precisely the hero; all of them are constrained by their place in the hierarchy, capable of cruelties they can hardly acknowledge because of their rank, and yet open to sudden transformations and escapes. Instead of a quest or a conflict that forms a thread through the imagined world, it's the oppressive richness of that world itself that's gripping: it's as though the writer's attention is inverted from the usual focus on people and events and turned instead on the inert mass of the surrounding and penetrating civilization in all its particularity. Often the characters do little but ponder these same things, before a spasm of action takes them; their actions often have effects opposite to what they hoped for, or come to nothing and leave them as they were.

The three books struck me when I first read them as an ideal kind of fantasy: one that was largely, in some sense solely, about an invented world—a world of a complexity equal to or surpassing our own, whose laws can't be entirely known but whose physical and social constraints cause certain kinds of lives to be lived. A world like the one we inhabit, the world that SF and fantasy writers call the "shared" world: complex, irreducible, indifferent or hostile to human success. In teaching the writing of fantasy and SF I sometimes ask students to read accounts of real civilizations and cultures in this shared world, from voodoo societies to North Korean totalitarianism to Romany social practices and Tibetan religion: I want them to see that invented worlds should seem at least as elaborated and rich as the ones we humans have actually created, though they rarely are.

Park went on to write a series of unique novels that might seem to fit various common rubrics but actually don't: an unsettling and original alien-encounter novel (*Cælestis*); the fantasia on the life of Jesus, who gains his enlightenment and his teachings from Himalayan Buddhists (*The Gospel of Corax*); and a further take on the Jesus story which earns its intensity by an absolute and startling this-worldness (*Three Marys*). All of them earned insightful reviews and thoughtful praise as well as a measure of incomprehension and dismissal. Then (besides a number of unclassifiable tales, some included in the present volume) he undertook another multi-part fantasy, resembling but going far beyond the first.

The series is called collectively *A Princess of Roumania*—the spelling is significant—and so is the first volume, which qualifies as the common fantasy form identified by the great taxonomist of the fantastic John Clute as a *portal fantasy*: the kind where people pass out of the shared or common world into a different one via a portal or gate or other egress—a wardrobe in C.S. Lewis's Narnia tales, a rabbit hole and a mirror in Lewis Carroll's. Park's setting at first is a college town in the Berkshires, recognizably Williamstown, where Miranda, a girl of twelve, lives with her adopted parents, hangs out with her new friend Peter (who was born with only one arm) and her racier girlfriend Andromeda. She was born in Romania [*sic*], and her adoptive parents took her at age eight from one of the hellish orphanages of the Ceausescu era. She came with a few possessions, one of which was a book, written in Romanian, seeming to have come from some long-ago time of wealth and luxury. It, and a bracelet of tiger's heads and a few coins, had been given to her new parents by the orphanage.

Books as portals aren't unusual in fantasies; it's a kind of primitive metafiction whereby a character in a book can escape into a book in the book, and find it real (Michael Ende's *The Neverending Story*, e.g.). Park leads us for a time to suppose that this is what will happen to Miranda, that in the book she'll find her real home. But a strange gang of punk teenagers speaking Romanian steals the book from her and throws it into a bonfire. And instantly the pleasant world of Massachusetts, the famous art museum, the Price Chopper, the nice old houses and the college, vanish away. Miranda and her friends are in a different America: the real, untamed America. We come to learn that Massachusetts and our twentieth century existed only in the book, a haven to keep Miranda safe, created by her alchemist aunt Aegypta Schenk von Schenk in the great and powerful state of Roumania far away. Miranda doesn't merely travel from the common world to a different one, like Harry Potter; her real world was always unreal, and now is destroyed. It's a daring device—daring because all readers, particularly those like me who live there, know that Massachusetts is, outside of this book, still very real.

Her two friends Peter and Andromeda are with her—they are actually companions assigned by her aunt to protect her, and only seemed to be American teenagers. Peter is Pieter de Graz, a seasoned soldier; Andromeda is a dog—though that's not all she is. Peter has a new arm, the arm of a stronger, older man. All three will struggle to remember the Massachusetts they lost, but now for them America is a vast woodland, barely touched by Europeans. In time they are captured by Roumanian scouts sent to find them, and they begin a long hard trek through the wilderness toward the Albany trading post, the ocean and Roumania.

Simultaneously we are in Great Roumania, where several parties are tracking by occult means Miranda's progress. The Baroness Ceausescu discovers a book like the one burned in the false Massachusetts, a book detailing a history of Roumania she rejects, full of Nazis and Soviet armies and a different Ceausescu regime, gloomy and squalid. *Her* Bucharest is the grand capital of a multiethnic country that hasn't experienced our twentieth century. Nor has the world around it, where North Africa ("Abyssinia") is the source of technical innovations and scientific progress, the British Isles and France were destroyed by a massive tsunami long before, there is a Tsar in Russia and a Sultan in Turkey, temples to Venus and Diana are the cathedrals and basilicas, and the many religions are conflated and deformed by (real) history into wonderful strangeness: "[Ludu Rat-tooth] told the story of Jesus of Nazareth, how he led the slaves to revolution on the banks of the Nile. Afterward he led his armies into Italy. He crucified the captured generals before the walls of Rome." His warrior queen, Mary Magdalene, brought the Gypsies out of Egypt (so the Gypsies believe). Below this world is the hidden world, from which occult powers spring and humans are subsumed in their archetypes.

Such transmogrifications are common enough in alternative-world novels, though the extravagance and specificity of these is striking. What makes these four volumes unique is that the inventions are not dealt out to us as needed to make scenes or stage the plot, nor to form the background of the adventures of Miranda on her way to her destiny. They are the integument of the book as much as—perhaps more than—the course of the action is.

Descriptions, tones, a writer's constant production of things—clothing and buildings and foodstuffs but also thoughts, momentary sensations, variations of sunlight and weather—these are what make the world of a fiction real, they are the metonymic medicines of actuality. In realistic ("mimetic") stories and novels they have value only if they go toward making actual this family home, this city, this job, this restaurant, this love affair; those that do not are effectually nonexistent. Fantasy literature is different—much of what the author provides is particular to an invented realm while at the same time familiar, having symbolic rather than metonymic power—swords, chalices, crowns, steeds—that abstract readers from their familiar actualities. The strange thing is how few novels sold as fantasy-realm series and listed alongside Park's contain enough such things, and load all their power into events, quests and conflicts that readers of such stories have encountered many times before. Park's Roumania series—to a much greater degree even than the Starbridge books—is as dense with synecdochic detail as the great realist novels of the place and time in which (*mutatis* very much *mutandis*) it is set, and almost requires the constant attention that an obdurate self-creating modernist text requires. It's like reading *A Man without Qualities* or Proust or late Henry James, not because these books resemble those books at all, but because they make a similar demand on the attention and on the reader's powers of appreciation, and the risk of surfeit that reading them entails—you, or at least I, can only read in them for so long before having to pause. Keep up, the text seems to say, every word of this is meant, it's neither page-filling nor self-indulgence, some of it will be answered in later pages and some not but that's not the reason to pay attention.

There's no doubt that a certain inspiration came to Park from Philip Pullman's inventive series *His Dark Materials*, which basically initiated the current young-girl-born-to-greatness mode. Park may have got from Pullman the animal forms that inhabit his characters, which escape from the body at death (though such inner forms have further life and purposes in the hidden world). But Pullman's *narrative* is as unsurprising and off-the-shelf as his world is imaginative and new. It progresses—as does Tolkien's—by a steady alternation of scenes of threat, danger, discomfort, and ignorance, and scenes of warmth, relief, and intimations of resolution; each scene is like a brick put in place in a growing edifice, whose shape and reason come clearer and clearer to us. There's no such rhythm to Park's series. Some of the most memorable scenes have very little to do with the evolving dynastic epic or Miranda's transformation into the long-awaited "white tyger" who will save her nation from German hegemony. A long episode in which the wandering Pieter de Graz is falsely accused of an inconsequential murder and brought before a grotesque Turkish magistrate, who forces him to participate in a wrestling competition or be execut-ed, is Kafkaesque in its intensity and absurd detail, yet effectu-ally comes to nothing. It's among the most haunting scenes in the work, haunting the way dreams haunt waking life.

Park's continuous production of small and large descriptions of the things and circumstances of his Great Roumania, the nu-ances of ethnic difference, the names of officials, hereditary and military titles, architecture, interiors, food and drink, hierarchies of speech—an almost hypnagogic flow of imagery—embed his characters as though in a highly researched historical novel. In fact one of the pleasures of the book is the recurrent remembrance that these things never did and never could have happened. This weird authenticity extends to the people: the Baroness Ceausescu is the evil force, the manipulative wicked fairy of the book, and yet in her belief in her own basic goodness—that she is alone and helpless and does only what she must, that others must see her as innocent and wronged—she is weirdly touching, an af-fect she understands and regularly deploys. Her great opponent, in the world of the living and in the hidden world, is Aegypta Schenk, Miranda's aristocratic aunt, gentle yet iron-willed. When the Baroness seeks her out at her hidden shrine of Venus in the woods, her rage, self-pity, self-exculpation, and finally murder proceed not only through speech and action but through the things and nature of the place. Partial quotation can only suggest the power of this lengthy scene:

"You will talk to me," she said. She knelt over the princess with the stiletto in her hand. She pressed the point into her spotted neck under the knot of the white cord, but didn't prick her. Then, suddenly disgusted with herself, she got to her feet and put the dagger down on the ledge of the hearth. She had a headache from the brandy and whatever was in the tea, and she was breathing hard. "I won't let you," she said. Then to calm herself, she threw some more wood on the fire and started to explore the house.

This was the larger room with the fireplace and the armchairs, the table and benches. The princess cooked on a primus stove. There was a food cupboard set into the wall. Opened, it revealed a plethora of delicacies: marmalade, cornichons, olives, pickled cherries, sardines, smoked oysters, teas. Many of the bottles and cans had foreign labels.

"You know it's true, what I told you," the baroness said. "I came from a village near Pietrosul. Seven of us in a room. Not like this—we had nothing. Just a wooden shack in the mountains. Water from the stream. Cold in the winter, I remember. Oh, I remember . . ."

Her guilt at the princess's murder will only increase her undying hatred and resentment, and—because this is not a historical fiction or a mimetic one—she will have to face Aegypta's opposition from the hidden world forever.

The most puzzling character in the series is the central one, Miranda Popescu, whose nature is a puzzle to herself, and whose actions in the world of Great Roumania are for a long time tentative and irresolute. She behaves, in other words, like an American teenage girl reborn in these impossibilities, having lost everything—a refugee, in effect, with a young person's tentative allegiances and inability to be entirely whole. For a long time she suffers more than she acts, and follows more than she leads. Some readers have expressed impatience with this, and yet it is realistic in a way rare in this kind of fiction, wherein to be thrown into a different world is usually a test to be passed, and that is passed with dispatch. She grows by leaps—that is, in this realm she has sudden years magically added to her age, and by the end is no longer a teenager at all but a young woman. Her soul-growth is slower, though, and her stature at the end is correspondingly great. At the end she is offered—or creates for herself—a choice of realms, and takes the harder.

There is another key to Miranda, though, which leads me back to Park's story collection where this present consideration began. The second volume of the series, *The Tourmaline*, is dedicated to "Miranda, of course," and it's easy to find out that Paul Park's daughter is named Miranda, that she was born a few years before the Roumania series was begun (which makes her now about the age of Miranda Popescu at the time of the last volume), and that Park was born and lived in Williamstown amid the scenes where the book begins, to which it now and then returns in memory, and where it nearly ends. Of course—as noted above—a lot of books derive power from the author's life; but a dedication to a daughter whose name is the name of the titular character, in a novel set in the town where author and daughter lived and that he causes to vanish like a dream—all that suggests metafiction. And in fact his work since the completion of the series has moved far and fast in that direction.

His next substantial publication was *All Those Vanished Engines*, comprising three intertwining novellas that would take almost as long to adequately describe as to read. It contains fictional versions of himself (a character writes the novel that Paul Park has written for the *Dungeons & Dragons* franchise) and various relations, including ancestors real and imagined that he places in the post–Civil War period in an America invaded by aliens, aliens who also invade in the future of that past—at least in the stories of a future writer who is imagined into being by one of those ancestors. And it includes an anti-history of the titanic machines housed in the buildings of the former Sprague Electric Company in North Adams (a few miles from Williamstown), which now comprise the Massachusetts Museum of Contemporary Art (Mass MoCA), for which Park wrote an interactive exhibit about an alien spaceship. It's the constant transformations and evanescences of *Roumania*, now bound up with a real lived life. I have wondered how much the effect of it depends on the reader's knowledge of these extra-literary things; it actually doesn't entirely exist without them.

"I don't want to think too hard, in this context, of the parasitic nature of the writer's relationship to his or her subject," Park says, in a note to one of the stories in *Other Stories*, a remark that suggest he thinks about it quite a lot. "The Blood of Peter Francisco" in the volume is a retro-noir story set in the same—or similarly distorted—world as the mad post-bellum one in *All Those Vanished Engines*; this would be evident to any reader of both, but only with Park's note do we get the family history buried in it.

Autobiographical-metafictional in an entirely different way (or perhaps no way at all) is in "No Traveler Returns," dedicated to a dead friend, Jim Charbonnet, "who was going to help me with the ending": the same dedication, in the same words, appears in the first volume of the Roumania series. This story, though, which begins with Park at Charbonnet's bedside as he lies dying, becomes a series of fanfold adventures involving yetis, mad monks in Tibet, beautiful women from his friend's life, places he had promised to accompany him to, to which he now goes to battle evil agents, be taken prisoner, escape, nearly die, etc., on and on in a remarkable tour de force of continuously collapsing narrative that revolves but never resolves. It can't be separated from the dying, then dead, then not dead dedicatee appearing and disappearing until the end; it would lose much of its hilarity and strangely touching power without the actuality described in the notes that form an integral and integrating part of this volume.

Readers acquiring it will get plenty more, including "Three Visits to a Nursing Home," the central panel of the triptych that makes up *All Those Vanished Engines*, and a terrific Poe pastiche set in New Orleans. It's common for a reviewer familiar with his subject to recommend a book of stories as a sort of tasting menu before embarking on the author's big work. Witty, original, and beautifully written as many of these stories are, though, I think the way to read Park is to begin right off with *A Princess of Roumania*. Afterward there will be room for all the rest. Unless the reader is the sort who, having finished the four Roumania volumes, will want to immediately begin again—or, because it is that kind of work, to simply open a volume anywhere and start to read, and be taken up in a world as thick as her own but not her own.

"I Did Crash a Few Parties"
John Crowley interviewed by Terry Bisson

You received the World Fantasy Award for Life Achievement in 2006, yet you are still with us. What went wrong?

Mario Puzo once remarked, after getting a $400,000 advance on *The Godfather*, that an amount of money like that (it was worth lots more at the time than now) was like finding out you don't have to die. I'm wondering if you can win a Lifetime Achievement Award over and over without end.

Like many ambitious, eager, overly self-confident wannabes from the provinces (I'm one myself) you bolted for New York as soon as you graduated to long pants. What party were you hoping to crash? Any luck?

I went to New York from Indiana. There were two directions ambitious artistic/literary types could go then, to New York or to Los Angeles. I wanted to make movies, not write fiction (I'd done that), but I chose New York. The films made in New York were "underground" movies, and I saw a lot of them. I wrote what are now called pitches, also scripts, with an old Indiana chum—Lance Bird, who was more passionate about filmmaking than I was—and in the end I did work in film, but in documentary—historical docs made from old film, a job I loved. I did crash a few parties, too. At that time it was nearly impossible for anyone living in certain neighborhoods or going to certain bars (Max's Kansas City) not to brush up against famous people or people once famous or about to become famous.

Ever cross paths with the Warhol crowd in those days?

My first New York job was as a photographer's assistant to a big fashion/advertising studio photographer of a kind that hardly exists any longer. He shot fashion spreads for *Life* magazine, and the *Life* fashion editor thought that a shoot using underground movies as backgrounds would be cool. So as the resident young hip person I was sent up to the Factory to collect the reels from Paul Morrissey, who was about to become a filmmaker in his own right. I had tried to explain that Warhol's films were stunningly boring (that was the point, of course) and that Jack Smith's *Flaming Creatures* or the Kuchar brothers' *Sins of the Fleshapoids* would be better, but *Life* mostly used Warhol's *Empire* and *Sleep*. At a party afterward one of the editorial women told me she was going to "get" Andy. I listened as she told him a story about the famous Art Market show where the paintings were set up as in a grocery store (including Wayne Thiebaud's cakes and Andy's Campbell's Soup). Buyers took away their purchases in grocery-store shopping bags. She'd got one— they were signed by Warhol—and her son, she said, had thought it was just a paper bag and took it to school with his books in it!

Warhol, po-faced as always, murmured, "Oh, that's wonderful." The woman was a little put off by this, and said, "But here's the thing—the bag fell apart on the way! It was a lousy bag!" Warhol was almost thrilled. "Oh, that's so wonderful, is that really true? Oh, you must tell that story to Henry [Geldzahler, the critic, who was at the party]," and he pulled her over to meet him. Andy was un-beardable.

Unlike many of your Grub Street colleagues, you are a member of the prestigious American Academy of Arts and Letters. Is the food any good?

At the one luncheon I was invited to, it was quite nice. Jackie Kennedy, Philip Roth, and others were there. I have never been asked back. Actually I'm not a member, or a fellow, or whatever; I was given an award in literature that year along with Roth and the wonderful Vicki Hearne (*Adam's Task*). There was real money attached. Harold Bloom was on the prizes committee that year. I was quite poor. The name has changed, and now you must say The American Academy and Institute of Arts and Letters.

What's the deal with The Girlhood of Shakespeare's Heroines *(which is rather hard to find)? What's its relationship to the nineteenth-century classic by Mary Cowden Clarke?*

It was published by a small press (Subterranean) as a limited edition, and reprinted in the famed "New Weird" issue of *Conjunctions*, the Bard College literary magazine. How hard to find can that be? Actually I'm hoping to make it easier to find soon—I'm working on a book of my uncollected stories, and this is one. (Another will be the story whose first appearance is in this PM book.) Mary Cowden Clarke's book, which I have, and have looked into, was described to me by John Hollander as a "very common romance type of the late nineteenth century," though he didn't describe the type further. It tells made-up (i.e., baseless) tales of the, yes, childhoods of Shakespeare's heroines—how Beatrice won over a gang of robbers, how Juliet's mother came into possession of the poison that later Juliet uses, and so forth. The language is sort-of-Shakespearean. The book's long. In my piece (which originally was simply called "Avon") the title is used to describe an aspiring teenage actress who contracts polio and is a heroine in several senses. She and the boy in love with her come upon the book in the library of a small town in Indiana, where there is (though there really wasn't) a Shakespeare festival in the 1960s.

You wrote the "Easy Chair" column in Harper's *for a while. How did that come about? Do you have a different discipline and approach for fiction and nonfiction?*

Christopher Beha, who was then coeditor of the magazine, liked my novels, wrote a fine review in *Bookforum* about them. When I was asked to do a reading at the 92nd St. Y in New York I was told I needed an introducer, and I asked Chris. *Harper's* later published a lecture I did about Utopia in the front matter of the magazine, and a review of a biography of Madame Blavatsky (very fun). When I found I needed an operation on a failing heart valve and would lose a semester's teaching (and the accompanying income), I called Chris and asked if maybe I could submit some article ideas, and—to my astonishment—he asked if I wanted to do the "Easy Chair" every other month. Saved my ass, in effect. (He hadn't known about the operation; he just thought I'd be good at it.)

I don't know about a different discipline. My fiction often depends on an authorial voice telling things—not only stories but facts and thoughts—to the reader; a lot of it is drawn out of research on all kinds of things. So are the columns. I felt a great freedom, and at the same time a fear: were these subjects and their treatment really interesting to anybody? Why did I think I had a claim on readers' attention? Chris (who, sadly for me but not for him, is no longer at the magazine) was uniformly encouraging.

What are the Least Trumps?

If you think I am going to allow myself a cheap joke in answer to this ("the ones he hides in his hairpiece" etc.) you mistake me. The Least Trumps—that is, a deck of cards with mystic or allegorical pictures having connections to the story—appeared in my first novel, *The Deep*. The images and mottoes on the cards were inspired by Renaissance magic images described by Frances Yates in her book *The Art of Memory*. The deck that various persons in *Little, Big* lay out has picture cards that are more like the Greater Trumps of the Tarot deck than the Renaissance images. Great-aunt Cloud—the character in the book who uses them most—calls them the Least Trumps because all they seem to answer are questions about small events of daily life—whether it will rain on a picnic or if a cold will get worse—though in the end they are discovered to be Great after all. Charles Williams's 1932 mystic novel is called *The Greater Trumps*.

Why are there so many John Crowleys in IMDb? Which one are you?

I recently went to see the fine film *Brooklyn* and at the end was pleasantly disoriented at seeing my name loom up amid the titles, all alone and about nine feet long. If only. Of course he is the Irish film and stage director, living the life I should have had instead of this one as an ink-stained wretch.

Another John Crowley (with middle initial W, inverting my own middle M) teaches American history at Syracuse. When we communicated once to untangle a confusion that had arisen about which of us wrote what—our bibliographies had gotten mixed together in Wikipedia—he told me that he'd had a student who went to Syracuse specifically to study with John Crowley, that is with me. Sorry I missed him.

My filmography is long but most of it wouldn't be on IMDb.

Perhaps your best-known documentary film has a definite science fiction feel, The World of Tomorrow. *Who is Lance Bird?*

Lance Bird (yes, his real name, though in an [unpublished] *roman à clef* about the movie scene in NYC in the 1970s the author gave him the name Blaise Falcon.) The real Bird's middle name is Evan, which allowed me to make the neat and similarly absurdly romantic anagram Nic Ravenblade. Lance and I were at Indiana University together. We both wanted to make films, but he had already worked on a micro-budget horror film that was finished and exhibited in a couple of theaters. We both took photography classes (on the principle that the lenses and the film were the same) and set out to make an underground film (this term is getting too constant here) with the IU photography department's wind-up Bolex 16mm camera. It was never finished but was to be called *Tigers in Lavender*—I had read somewhere that tigers respond to lavender plants the same way cats respond to catnip. Lance moved to NYC too and spent his time trying to get scripts read and deals made; I collaborated on the scripts. That never happened, but Lance began working with a partner, Tom Johnson, on documentaries about auto racing, beginning with stock cars and then Le Mans–style endurance racing. I wrote narration for some of these, despite the fact that I had not learned to drive and had never had a license (and me a Hoosier, sort of!).

In the late '70s the NEH began giving away lots of money for work in TV, and the three of us made a documentary that started as a study of Walker Evans and became a story of the whole Depression. And then *The World of Tomorrow*, about the 1939 World's Fair, which is a weird kind of masterpiece (my wife calls it my "secret fiction film"). Working with Lance and Tom I acquired my love of archival film and the strange metaphysics of making movies with dead people walking and talking, sometimes about the world to come.

The famed critic Harold Bloom dragged you from the Den of Obscurity that is the birthright of every SF/Fantasy author. Have you forgiven him?

I'm not sure how much less obscure I am. But I owe Harold Bloom much. The connection had an odd beginning: I had never read his criticism, though I knew his name and fame, and once in the library I picked up his book *Agon*, which has a long essay in it on what he calls heroic fantasy. It was so illuminating and interesting that I wrote him a letter—I'd never written to an academic critic—and sent along a book of mine that I thought reflected his views (it was *Engine Summer*). Pretty soon he wrote back and said he'd read it, was moved by it, and had gone to the library and picked up some other books of mine and read them too. *Little, Big* was the one that touched him most, and he has never ceased to praise it to anyone nearby. His sponsorship got me the half-time teaching job at Yale I still hold.

Like many SF/Fantasy authors, you teach writing. Do you actually have a method or are you winging it?

Isn't winging it a method? I talk mostly about the shapes and forms of fiction, the machinery that generates all kinds of stories. I don't instruct them as to what *sort* of fiction I think is good or not good; I try my best to discover what they want to achieve and try to help. I have one great advantage at Yale—creative writing classes require applications with writing samples, and from thirty to fifty applications I can choose a class of twelve. So I get not only good or promising writers but ones I think I can help. I had no idea when I began how much I would enjoy teaching—mostly for the chance to be with young people and know their thoughts. I know more about how a certain (but broad) class of twenty-year-olds thinks than a great majority of people my age. Next spring, 2018, will be my last semester.

Bloom praised your "superb and sustained elusiveness," and I join him in that. But I sometimes wonder, commercially, is it a feature or a fault?

Oh jeez. There is a nearly ontological difficulty here. I think I am elusive sometimes, but I also think I lay tracks (though sometimes I brush them away). I really want readers to follow, to play the game I'm setting up. At the same time I understand that a large percentage of the general reading public has little interest in such agonistic labor or pleasure. And I also want many many readers, both to enhance my self-esteem and make me money to live on. And (again) I want my work to please me in its multiplicity and its interconnections, formed sometimes by the repetition of a single word in differing circumstances. I keep believing that I have written a book *this* time that everyone can like, or at least millions can like, and it will make me honored and rich, and I keep on queering the deal by my usual elusiveness, peculiarity, literariness (by which I mean that the secret subtext of my works is always *this is a book*), and general self-pleasing. Oh well.

What's the deal with The Chemical Wedding?

The Chemical Wedding, by Christian Rosencreutz (the actual author was a German theology student named Johann Valentin Andreae) is a sort of romance written in 1616 about a self-doubting and anxious but essentially good man who receives an invitation to a wedding in a magic castle. It's usually regarded as some sort of allegory, maybe of the alchemical process (a lot of alchemical sort of stuff goes on in it, and some of the characters could stand for alchemical stages), but at bottom I think it's a mad sort of novel, using the farthest-out technologies and sciences of the time. It might also be a parody of those sciences and technologies. I have loved it for years, and I did a new version (not a translation) that

I hoped would make it more accessible to readers. In trying to describe what sort of thing it is, I created (unintentionally) something of a stir by describing it as a candidate for the first science fiction novel. Complaints were made that the "science" in it was unscientific (Kepler and Galileo were the real scientists of the time) and that you can't have science fiction based on bogus guesswork science. I imagine such critics hadn't read much early SF.

You once spoke in an interview of your "compassion for characters in novels—who live in a world that has a shape that they don't know and can't finally alter." Hmmm. Equally true for Little, Big *and for* Four Freedoms? *Is it a feature of The Novel in general?*

I think it is a feature. Just as we ignore unwelcome or difficult facts in our actual lives—personal and public and universal facts—we ignore the absolute fact that the characters in the novels we read have made all their decisions, errors, triumphs, before we start to read the book. The end that they will come to, which determines all that they will do in the story, is fixed—the book's in print! Of course writers can fall in love with a character in the course of the writing and find themselves unwilling finally to subject them to the endings planned for them—but even so, the endings are the endings and can't be changed when the book's done.

Little, Big and *Four Freedoms* seem to differ in that in the first there's a tale being told whose shape is finally revealed, which all the human characters learn they have been enacting all along, and who exit that tale as the book ends. In the second, nothing seems fixed, and characters come upon new openings and new turnings they can't have imagined; nevertheless they come to an ending in which they are as fixed as the archetypes they embody on the last page. If you'd like to read more of my thoughts on the subject you could go to *Harper's* magazine and look for my "Easy Chair" essay called "A Ring-shaped World."

Ever get a bad review? One that helped?

I've actually had very few bad reviews. I've wondered if this is because reviewers who are among the small band of committed readers of my books somehow manage to get the review copies and submit positive reviews. The vast number of bad reviews I seem to collect on Amazon (along with vast numbers of moderate, disappointed, confused, ecstatic, and unintelligible ones) suggests something of the kind. The worst review I ever got was in the *New York Times*, when they used to run short "also noticed" reviews. It was for *Dæmonomania*, the third volume of a four-volume novel, and the reviewer was apparently unaware of this fact. He was puzzled and annoyed and found the book both silly and tortured.

Reviews that helped? Long ones, like Chris Beha's mentioned, or James Hynes's in the *Boston Review*. If for nothing but to learn if what I wrote was intelligible, if my general purpose was understood.

Do you still write for film? Ever try a narrative (fiction) feature? How is writing for documentaries different?

I have been working with Laurie Block, who is my wife, on a biography of Helen Keller for *American Masters* (PBS). It's been in the works now for a long time, but there are signs it may soon be headed for completion. I cowrote the script (it was a heavily scripted show, much of it based on Keller's writings, spoken by the great Cherry Jones—not portraying Keller but giving us Keller's written words). I've long since given up trying to write fiction films; it's easier to write a novel of a movie idea—at least you have *something* in the end. (None of my novels have been sold to the movies, though there was some interest in a couple.) Now I'm looking into the possibility of *Little, Big* being a "premium TV" project with multiple seasons. More on that in some possible future where there is more.

Most documentaries have minimal writing; when I began writing those historical docs in the 1970s I took as my model the 1930s–40s docs like *The River* and *The Plow That Broke the Plains* and *Night Mail* (with narration by W.H. Auden!). Since sound recording was so clumsy then, most of the work of explication came through an intimate, characterized voice, sometimes even speaking in a (manufactured) present tense—that's how I wrote *The World of Tomorrow*, with Jason Robards in effect playing a character. Today all of that is unnecessary (as you can shoot a nice doc with your smartphone) and unwanted.

One sentence on each, please: Trollope, Lovecraft, Western Mass.

I have read almost no Trollope; my mother was delighted by him, but the conventionality of his writing and the kinds of things his innumerable books are concerned with are largely uninteresting to me.

I have read almost no Lovecraft; high school nerds I knew were delighted by him, and some people I know admire and cherish him, but the absurd extravagance of his writing, and his inability despite that extravagance to convey actual human feeling in extremity, make him uninteresting and in fact repellent to me.

I love Western Massachusetts, where my children were born, to which I fled from a decaying New York City in 1977, where I now live in a house forty minutes from where my conscious life began seventy years ago in southern Vermont, and where I live among all kinds of people, rich and poor, back-to-the-landers and never-left-the-landers, pickup drivers and Prius drivers—about as close to a practical Utopia as it's possible to get and still live in the ordinary.

*You often (*Little, Big *and* Ægypt*) write about arcane and conspiratorial religious orders that secretly control not only our lives but our realities. Do you know something that we don't?*

There is much that I know, Terry. Actually, not so much. I can't say why I am so attracted to stories and circumstances where thought and notions have power over the human realm and the natural order. It's noticeable, though, how few real believers in the kinds of gnostic mythologies I retail are interested in my writing, and how the few I have met that are attracted to it get it wrong. The best example of what I attempt is in the fabulously long Ægypt Cycle: through three volumes the gnostic realm both of hope and terror continually grows, the world is posited as being labile and able to undergo shifts of reality that human souls can influence. In the last volume the final shift or change is into the common world that the non-gnostics among us (in fact all of us) actually live in: "the Great Instauration of everything that had all along been the case." It occasioned some disappointment, though this conclusion was implicit in everything that went before.

You write about poets (Lord Byron); do you write poetry? Do you read it for fun? What about James Merrill (who blurbed one of your books)?

I assembled a personal anthology of poets and poems in my early years and it's basically lasted the rest of my life. Small additions have been made over time (I like John Ashbery very much, and James Merrill, yes). I wrote my last poem somewhere around 1975, and there weren't many in the previous decade—though masses of it in my teens and early twenties, most of it now well lost. But I don't read much modern poetry at all. I wrote a novel about a poet (*The Translator*) in part because a poet—Thomas M. Disch, my friend Tom—said that a poet would make a great hero for a bestseller. Americans, he averred, *love* poets even though they don't read poetry. I loved writing the book—and writing the poems in it, mostly the early poems of my heroine, and the translations she makes of the supposedly Nobel-worthy poems in Russian of her mentor. That was great fun. (It's another gnostic-gods-and-angels novel that puzzled people and came nowhere near being a bestseller.)

At Yale you teach a course in utopias, yet you've never attempted one. Or have you?

I think *Four Freedoms*, my World War II home front novel, is a sort of ambiguous utopia. The gigantic (imagined) factory, the care for the workers at all levels, the welcome to women, people of color, Native Americans; the money spent and the effort expended to make workplaces healthy and safe (they were neither by modern standards, but the effort was real); the provision of nurseries, clinics, information, recreation—well, I probably exaggerate all that, as utopias tend to do. At a point late in the book a woman who has won a management job in the factory wonders why the model provided by this factory, and by the astonishing productivity of industry in war, couldn't be simply continued in peacetime, producing cars and refrigerators and radios for everyone. She imagines something like a nationwide telephone tree that would let the government know who needed what.

In our title piece "Totalitopia" I present a glimpse of a socialist utopia with a world government, a distribution system like Amazon's but owned by the world, and all people siblings. Lewis Lapham, the publisher of the quarterly where the article appeared, couldn't decide if I was kidding. Neither can I. I recently read somebody saying that all utopias are dystopias in disguise—I reject that, though examples are legion.

What's next?

I have a new novel coming out from Saga in fall 2017. It was deliberately conceived to sell lots of copies, and because it's a frank fantasy I'm hoping it will win back the fantasy-fan readership I seem to have partly lost with the last couple of books. (To be clear, many readers of fantasy fiction also happily read books of other kinds, like mine.) The book is called *KA: Dar Oakley in the Ruin of Ymr.* Dar Oakley is a crow, born some two thousand years ago, who becomes involved with the human world and its otherworlds, and by mistake comes to possess a sort of immortality—he dies over and over but always comes back. He travels from somewhere in Celtic Europe to the American continent and lives in various societies through the centuries, up until some time in the future. Dar

Oakley learns to speak with various humans in many times and places, including one in near-future America who writes down his story. I've wanted to write a book about crows for years—for reasons obvious and not so—and here it is, or soon will be. I consider this my last full-dress novel—I'm very nearly as old as you—but my agent insists I never say that, so mum's the word.

What kind of car do you drive? (I ask this of everyone.)

My first car, acquired when I was thirty-six or so (I only learned to drive at that age), was an old American Motors Ambassador, a boat but a beaut. Next was a VW Dasher. A few others of indifferent lineage. Now a New England Hilltown Liberal Subaru.

The fairies in Little, Big *forget the past but remember the future. Were you remembering that Ted Chiang was someday going to be developing that idea for Hollywood?*

It's inappropriate for an interviewer to ask wittier questions than the subject can come up with answers for. Ted Chiang is much smarter than I am. His original story "Story of Your Life" is a marvel of syntactical invention which the movie based on it, *Arrival*, wonderful as it is, can't match.

Bibliography

Books

KA: Dar Oakley in the Ruin of Ymr (Saga, 2017). Novel.
The Chemical Wedding, by Christian Rosencreutz (Small Beer
      Press, 2016). Novel by Johann Valentin Andreae, in a new
      version by Crowley.
Four Freedoms (William Morrow, 2009). Novel.
In Other Words (Subterranean Press, 2006). Essays and criticism.
The Girlhood of Shakespeare's Heroines (Subterranean Press, 2005).
      Novella.
Lord Byron's Novel: The Evening Land (Morrow, 2005). Novel.
Novelties & Souvenirs: Collected Short Fiction (Morrow, 2004).
The Translator (Morrow, 2002). Novel.

The Ægypt Cycle:
Ægypt (Bantam Books/Spectra, 1987). Novel. Reissued as *The
      Solitudes* (Overlook Press, 2008).
Love & Sleep (Bantam, 1994). Novel.
Dæmonomania (Bantam, 2000). Novel.

Endless Things (Small Beer Press, 2007). Novel.

Antiquities (Incunabula, 1992). Stories.

Great Work of Time (Bantam/Spectra, 1990). Novella. World
    Fantasy Award, Best Novella, 1990.

Novelty (Doubleday/Foundation, 1989). Four stories: "Why the
    Nightingale Sings at Night," "In Blue," "Great Work of
    Time," "Novelty."

Little, Big (Bantam Books, 1981). Novel. World Fantasy Award,
    Best Novel, 1982.

Engine Summer (Doubleday, 1978). Science fiction novel.
    Nominated for the American Book Award. Reissued in
    Otherwise: Three Novels, Harper Perennial 1994.

Beasts (Doubleday, 1976). Science fiction novel. Reissued in
    Otherwise: Three Novels, Harper Perennial 1994.

The Deep (Doubleday, 1975). Science fiction novel. Reissued in
    Otherwise: Three Novels, Harper Perennial 1994.

Most of the books above have appeared in translation in
multiple languages.

Stories

(an incomplete list)

"The Million Monkeys of M. Borel," *Conjunctions* 67, Fall 2017.

"Spring Break," in *New Haven Noir*, ed. Amy Bloom (Akashic
    Books, 2017).

"Glow, Little Glowworm," *Conjunctions* 59, 2012.

Conversation Hearts chapbook edition (Subterranean Press, 2008).

"Little Yeses, Little Nos," *Yale Review*, April 2005.

"The Girlhood of Shakespeare's Heroines," *Conjunctions* 39, Fall 2002

An Earthly Mother Sits and Sings chapbook (Dream Haven Books, 2000).

"Gone," in *Fantasy & Science Fiction*, September 1996.

"Exogamy," in *Omni Best Science Fiction Three*, ed. Ellen Datlow (Omni Books, 1993).

"In Blue," in *The Year's Best Science Fiction Eighth Annual Collection*, ed. Gardner Dozois, 1991

"Missolonghi 1824," in *Poe's Children*, ed. Peter Straub (Doubleday, 2008 [orig. in *Asimov's*, 1990]).

"Snow," in *Omni*, 1985

"Novelty," in *American Fantastic Tales: Terror and the Uncanny from the 1940s to Now*, ed. Peter Straub (Library of America, 2009 [orig. 1983]).

"The Green Child," in *Elsewhere*, ed. Terry Windling, 1981.

"The Reason for the Visit," in *Interfaces*, ed. Ursula K. Le Guin and Virginia Kidd, 1980.

"Antiquities," in *Whispers*, ed. Stuart David Schiff, 1979.

"Where Spirits Gat Them Home," in *Shadows*, ed. Charles L. Grant, 1978.

"Novelty," in *Interzone*, Summer 1977.

"The Single Excursion of Caspar Last," in *Gallery*, September 1974.

"Somewhere to Elsewhere," in *The Little Magazine*, Spring 1974.

Stories have also appeared in the following anthologies, among others:

The Locus Awards (2004)

Masterpieces: Best Science Fiction of the Century (2001)

Future on Ice (1998)

Black Swan, White Raven (1997)

American Gothic Tales (1996)

Modern Classics of Fantasy (1996)

The Year's Best Fantasy and Horror (1994)

The Best from Fantasy and Science Fiction: The 50th Anniversary Anthology (1994)

The Norton Book of Science Fiction (1993)

Nebula Awards 25 (1991)

The Year's Best Fantasy and Horror Fourth Annual Collection (1991)

The Science Fiction Century (1988)

Terry Carr's Best Science Fiction of the Year 15 (1986)

Essays (Partial List)

Bimonthly essays for "The Easy Chair," *Harper's*, 2015–2016.

"Joan Aiken," *Boston Review*, December 2015.

"Angels and Demons," *Lapham's Quarterly*, Spring 2012.

"Unpacking" (review of Ben Katchor's *The Cardboard Valise*), *Boston Review*, November 2011.

"The Next Future," *Lapham's Quarterly*, Fall 2011.

"My Life in the Theater, 1910–1960" (memoir), *Yale Review*, January 2011.

"New Ghosts and How to Know Them," *Tin House* 47, Spring 2011.

Introduction to David Stacton, *The Judges of the Secret Court: A Novel about John Wilkes Booth* (New York Review Books, 2011).

"Blossom and Fade," *Lapham's Quarterly*, Summer 2010.

"Nicholson Baker," *Boston Review*, December 2009.

"In the Midst of Death," *Lapham's Quarterly*, Fall 2009.

"Uproars: Leslie Epstein's Magic," *Boston Review*, November 2008.

Introduction to Richard Hughes, *In Hazard* (New York Review Books, 2008).

"Rosamond Purcell," *Boston Review*, June 2007.

"Little Criminals: Three Rediscovered Novels by Richard Hughes," *Boston Review*, December 2005.

"The Happy Land" (review of Walt Kelly's *Pogo*, vols. 1–11), *Boston Review of Books*, October 2004.

"A Modern Instance: Magic, Imagination, and Power," *Journal of the Fantastic in the Arts* 12, no. 2, 2001.

Review of Ben Katchor's *The Jew of New York*, *Yale Review*, July 1999

"The Gothic of Thomas M. Disch," *Yale Review*, April 1995.

"The Labyrinth of the World and the Paradise of the Heart," *New York Review of Science Fiction*, November 1989.

About the Author

John Crowley was born in the appropriately liminal town of Presque Isle, Maine, the son of an Army Air Corps doctor, and eventually one of five children. Raised Catholic, he currently has no religious faith, though he's lately begun meditating regularly with no particular expectations.

He grew up in Vermont and then for a couple of years in coal-mining eastern Kentucky, thence to Indiana, where his father was the doctor of the student infirmary at Notre Dame, which John avoided attending.

After graduating from Indiana University he emigrated to New York City, where he worked at several occupations (photographer, publicist, proofreader of the Manhattan telephone book, television writer, hack). He began publishing novels in 1975 (*The Deep*). He received his exit visa from New York City in 1977 and moved to western Massachusetts, where he still lives with his wife of 35 years, and where his twin daughters were raised.

He is a recipient of the American Academy and Institute of Letters Award for Literature and the World Fantasy Lifetime Achievement Award. His novels include *Little, Big*; the Ægypt Cycle of magical history (*The Solitudes*, *Love & Sleep*, *Dæmonomania*, *Endless Things*); *The Translator* (winner of the Premio Flaiano Superprize, Italy); and *Lord Byron's Novel: The Evening Land*. His most recent novel is *Four Freedoms*, about building a giant (imagined) warplane in the 1940s; a new one, about Crows and death, will appear in Fall 2017. He teaches fiction writing and screenwriting at Yale University and will for another academic year.

Also available from PM Press

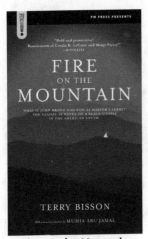

Sensation
NICK MAMATAS
ISBN: 978-1-60486-354-3
$14.95

Damnificados
JJ AMAWORO WILSON
ISBN: 978-1-62963-117-2
$15.95

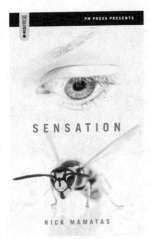

Fire on the Mountain
TERRY BISSON
Introduction by Mumia Abu-Jamal
ISBN: 978-1-60486-087-0
$15.95

Clandestine Occupations: An Imaginary History
DIANA BLOCK
ISBN: 978-1-62963-121-9
$16.95

Also available from PM Press

Gypsy
CARTER SCHOLZ
ISBN: 978-1-62963-118-9
$13.00

The Great Big Beautiful Tomorrow
CORY DOCTOROW
ISBN: 978-1-60486-404-5
$12.00

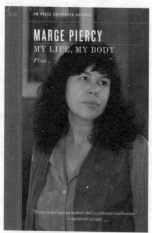

My Life, My Body
MARGE PIERCY
ISBN: 978-1-62963-105-9
$12.00

The Wild Girls
URSULA K. LE GUIN
ISBN: 978-1-60486-403-8
$12.00

Also available from PM Press

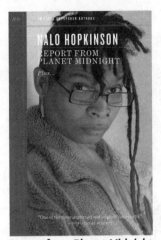

Report from Planet Midnight
NALO HOPKINSON
ISBN: 978-1-60486-497-7
$12.00

The Science of Herself
KAREN JOY FOWLER
ISBN: 978-1-60486-825-8
$12.00

Raising Hell
NORMAN SPINRAD
ISBN: 978-1-60486-810-4
$12.00

Fire.
ELIZABETH HAND
ISBN: 978-1-62963-234-6
$13.00

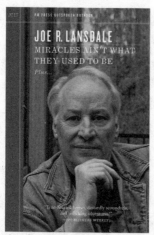
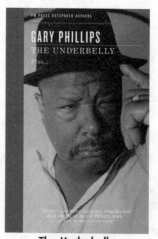

FRIEND OF
PM

These are indisputably momentous times—the financial system is melting down globally and the Empire is stumbling. Now more than ever there is a vital need for radical ideas.

In the years since its founding—and on a mere shoestring—PM Press has risen to the formidable challenge of publishing and distributing knowledge and entertainment for the struggles ahead. With hundreds of releases to date, we have published an impressive and stimulating array of literature, art, music, politics, and culture. Using every available medium, we've succeeded in connecting those hungry for ideas and information to those putting them into practice.

Friends of PM allows you to directly help impact, amplify, and revitalize the discourse and actions of radical writers, filmmakers, and artists. It provides us with a stable foundation from which we can build upon our early successes and provides a much-needed subsidy for the materials that can't necessarily pay their own way. You can help make that happen—and receive every new title automatically delivered to your door once a month—by joining as a Friend of PM Press. And, we'll throw in a free T-shirt when you sign up.

Here are your options:

- **$30 a month**: Get all books and pamphlets plus 50% discount on all webstore purchases
- **$40 a month**: Get all PM Press releases (including CDs and DVDs) plus 50% discount on all webstore purchases
- **$100 a month**: Superstar—Everything plus PM merchandise, free downloads, and 50% discount on all webstore purchases

For those who can't afford $30 or more a month, we have Sustainer Rates at $15, $10, and $5. Sustainers get a free PM Press T-shirt and a 50% discount on all purchases from our website.

Your Visa or Mastercard will be billed once a month, until you tell us to stop. Or until our efforts succeed in bringing the revolution around. Or the financial meltdown of Capital makes plastic redundant. Whichever comes first.

PM Press was founded at the end of 2007 by a small collection of folks with decades of publishing, media, and organizing experience. PM Press co-conspirators have published and distributed hundreds of books, pamphlets, CDs, and DVDs. Members of PM have founded enduring book fairs, spearheaded victorious tenant organizing campaigns, and worked closely with bookstores, academic conferences, and even rock bands to deliver political and challenging ideas to all walks of life. We're old enough to know what we're doing and young enough to know what's at stake.

We seek to create radical and stimulating fiction and nonfiction books, pamphlets, T-shirts, visual and audio materials to entertain, educate, and inspire you. We aim to distribute these through every available channel with every available technology—whether that means you are seeing anarchist classics at our bookfair stalls; reading our latest vegan cookbook at the café; downloading geeky fiction e-books; or digging new music and timely videos from our website.

PM Press is always on the lookout for talented and skilled volunteers, artists, activists, and writers to work with. If you have a great idea for a project or can contribute in some way, please get in touch.

PM Press
PO Box 23912
Oakland CA 94623
510-658-3906
www.pmpress.org